PERSONAL
Changes

—— THE *Personal* SERIES ——
K.C. WELLS

This is a work of fiction. Names, characters, places, and incidents either are the product of the author's imagination or are used fictitiously, and any resemblance to actual persons, living or dead, business establishments, events, or locales is entirely coincidental.

For Max Vos
Thank you for all those chats in Atlanta and via Skype
You were truly inspiring

and

Kol Anderson,
for being an ace writing partner and a damn good friend.

ACKNOWLEDGMENTS

Thanks, as always, to my wonderful betas,
Tina, Lara, Mardee and Max

Chapter One

"Morning, Boss." Rick greeted Blake with his usual cheerful grin. He helped himself to a coffee in the small kitchen that served their floor. "I didn't expect to see you in here today."

Blake tilted his head as he poured out two mugs of coffee. "And why would I be taking the day off?" He regarded Rick with amusement. "I don't recall the second of January being a national holiday, last time I looked."

Rick smirked. "Yeah, but after New Year's Eve I figured you and Will might have wanted a little time to yourselves. I mean, you did get engaged, right?" Rick waggled his eyebrows. "I'm sure you were both up late, seeing the New Year in." Another suggestive leer. "Among other things."

Blake paused mid-action and turned to face him. "Is this what I'm going to get every morning? The third degree about my private life?" The barest hint of a smile told Rick his boss hadn't really taken offense, but Rick knew Blake. It was time to back off.

His voice softened. "Sorry, Blake. And for the record, I think it's wonderful. You two make a beautiful couple." That much was true. Blake with his black hair and amazing blue eyes, and Will with dark, brown hair and those eyes the color of milk chocolate—they made a striking pair.

And I'm trying desperately to forget the fact that I've been lusting after you for six years.

The previous week's Christmas party had been

quite the night for revelations. When Rick had got over the shock that not only was his straight boss definitely *not* straight, he was also in love with his PA, Rick's first thought had been one of regret. When Blake had taken him on as part of his team, Rick had fallen in lust with him within a very short space of time. Of course, he'd never gone there—Rick had been burned enough times by making advances to straight guys to know that making a move on his dishy new boss would probably have had him out the door on his arse. It was bad enough that Will knew his secret.

"Aw, that's sweet." Will came into the kitchen and grinned at Rick, before taking the mug Blake handed him. "Thanks, babe."

Blake shot Will a warning glance. Will's grin faltered, until Blake patted his arm, smiled at them both and then exited the kitchen with his coffee mug. Will watched him go, an unreadable expression on his face.

"And what was that look all about?" Rick sensed a little tension in the air.

Will huffed. "We had a talk this morning, that's all, about my future here. Oh, and how we were going to play things from now on."

"Let me guess. Act professional, no being all lovey-dovey."

Will nodded glumly.

Rick chuckled. "I suppose that means you've seen the last of any shenanigans in his office."

Will groaned. "Oh God, don't remind me. Besides, he has a point. I mean, look what happened that last time he and I…"

He didn't have to finish. Blake's would-be

fiancée Melissa hadn't exactly caught them having sex in Blake's office, but had seen enough to make their lives miserable. At least she was out of the picture now. *And good riddance.*

Something Will had said finally registered. "Back up a minute. What do you mean, talking about your future here? You're not leaving, are you, Will?" Rick bit his lip. Will had only been with them for three months but in that time he'd become a good friend.

Will slurped his coffee and gave a low moan of appreciation. Blake made really good coffee. He warmed his hands on the mug. "Let's just say he's not happy about me continuing as his PA now we're engaged." Will scowled. "The jury is still out, however, on whether I quit. I don't want to—I still have my student loans to pay off, after all—but he says it's something we need to consider seriously."

Rick patted Will's arm. "Now don't you two fall out about this." Not that he could see much coming between the two men. Watching them together at the New Year's Eve party a couple of nights ago had been just beautiful. Rick had to admit, the two men really fitted each other. Never mind that it had only been three months since Will had strolled into Trinity Publishing and into Blake's life. *When you know, you know,* he reasoned with himself. *And the heart knows what it wants.*

Will smiled. "Don't worry about us. We'll sort it out, trust me." He levelled an intense stare at Rick. "But what about you? Made any New Year's resolutions?" He tilted his head. "And you know I'm talking about your love life here." His expression softened. "We need to find you a guy, Rick. I'm going to make it my mission this year." He gave a decisive nod.

Rick snorted. "Good luck with that."

Will's brow furrowed. "What do you mean?"

Rick let out a sigh and sipped his coffee. "I haven't been as lucky as you and Blake in that department. I seem to have lousy taste in men."

Will eyed him keenly. "Have you been looking? And if so, *where* have you been looking?"

Rick thought for a moment and then walked over to the door. He pushed it shut and leaned back against it. Will regarded him curiously.

"Look," Rick began, lowering his voice, "the longest relationship I've had lasted three months. Men don't seem to want to stick around me. So now I take what I can get."

"What does that mean?" Will's voice was suddenly as low as Rick's.

Rick expelled his breath. "It means I go to a lot of clubs and I have a lot of casual sex, okay?" His eyes met Will's. "That comment I made a while ago about being in toilet stalls with guys? I wasn't kidding." He lowered his gaze.

"Aw, Rick, I didn't know that's what you were doing." Will stepped closer and gave Rick a brief but firm hug. Rick closed his eyes. It had been a while since anyone had hugged him. When he opened them again, Will moved back and gave him a stern look. "I don't have to ask if you're being safe, do I?"

Rick's chest tightened. Will was a good friend. "No, you don't. I may be a slut, but I'm not stupid."

The crease between Will's eyes deepened. "I don't like it when you talk about yourself like that."

Rick shrugged. "I'm just being honest, that's all. I like sex, I'm not ashamed to admit that. And yes, every Friday and Saturday, you'll probably find me in a club, chatting up some bloke before going home with him or taking him back to mine." He met Will's gaze. "But if I found someone who wanted to do the whole monogamous route, someone who wanted us to be serious about each other?" He smiled. "I'd be off the club scene so fast, you'd get whiplash watching me leave." His heart felt heavy. "Right now, there doesn't seem to be anyone out there who wants me like that, so until then, I'll carry on being careful and always leaving my flat with a supply of condoms."

Will looked sad as Rick opened the door to go to his office, ready to start work, coffee mug still in his hand.

"I'm going to keep checking on you, all right?" Will said earnestly.

Rick blew him a kiss. "You're a sweet guy, Will, and Blake's a very lucky man." He paused in the doorway. "Thanks, mate. I'm glad we're friends."

"Always." Will's tone was serious. "And you can come talk to me anytime, you know that?" Rick nodded.

"Okay. Then get to work, lazybones." His eyes sparkled with good humour.

Rick tugged his hair in a subservient gesture. "Yes, sir. Right away, sir." He winked. "Got to keep in with the boss's boyfriend, after all." He ducked as Will picked up a tea towel and threw it at him, missing him by inches. Rick laughed and walked along the corridor to his office.

Time to get some work done. He had a host of advance review copies to send out to review sites, not to mention setting up time for authors to meet their readers on Trinity's Facebook page. He could get some of it done before Blake's morning team meeting. *No rest for the wicked.* And the way he was feeling right now? When Friday night got here, he intended being very wicked indeed.

G-A-Y was positively heaving. The dance floor was packed. Rick saw some couples dancing so close, he'd have been hard pressed to slide a cigarette paper between them. Then he snorted. *No difference there. Same ol' Friday night.*

"God, I'm run off my feet tonight," Erroll exclaimed as he passed Rick, tray held high laden with several glasses of different sizes and types. Rick liked Erroll. He wasn't into twinks, but the waiter was seriously cute, with big blue eyes. Rick was a sucker for blue eyes.

"Keeping you busy, then?" Rick grinned.

Erroll rolled his eyes. "Honey, it seems like half the gay guys in London decided to check us out." He flicked his head toward the stage. "Of course, that might have something to do with it. The number of fliers I've seen around advertising these boys is nobody's business."

Rick followed his gesture to where the cute boys in barely-there shorts gyrated around poles, one of whom seemed intent on proving to all concerned exactly how flexible he could be. Rick chuckled. "Oh my. He's going to have them lining up for a lap-dance later on." He patted Erroll on the back. "I'll let you get on."

Erroll flashed him a grateful smile and sashayed across the floor, flirting furiously with the customers as he passed them, his tight little arse wiggling. Rick admired the view.

"Haven't seen you here before," a low voice said beside him.

Rick turned to see a young man, probably in his mid-twenties, dressed in the tightest jeans Rick had ever seen, with a T-shirt depicting a moustached guy in leather gear, and a dark blue hoodie. Rich brown eyes in a beautiful face.

"Then I don't know where you've been," Rick said with a smile that he hoped was sexy. "I'm here a lot." He held out his hand. "The name's Rick."

"Hi, Rick." Those brown eyes flashed in appreciation. "I'm Oli." He gave a nod toward the bar. "And the gorgeous hunk over there in the black wife-beater is my other half, Ben."

Rick followed his nod and caught his breath when he saw Ben. The guy was seriously ripped and that black top did little to hide it. Dark-skinned compared to Oli's creamy complexion, they made a beautiful couple. "Fuck me," Rick muttered under his breath as he watched Ben moving sinuously to the music whose beat pulsed through the club. *That's one hot man. Actually, make that* two *hot men…*

To his surprise Oli edged closer until his breath wafted over Rick's neck. "Oh, trust me, babe, that's what I had in mind." He slid his tongue into Rick's ear and a frisson of excitement rippled down Rick's spine.

"Aren't…aren't you two…I mean, do you…" The slow movement of Oli's tongue over his ear lobe and down his neck was robbing Rick of all coherent thought.

Oli stopped his teasing motion and whispered into Rick's ear. "We like to play, babe. Never on our own though, always together." Oli stroked Rick's arm, the touch light yet very sensual. "But when we share a guy? It can get pretty wild." He paused. "Does that sound like something that might interest you?" The words tickled Rick's ear. He nodded, shivering. "What say we sit down over there in the corner booth and get acquainted?"

Rick didn't need a second invitation. "Let's go."

Oli led the way to the corner and pushed Rick into the seat, his back to the wall, and then sat next to him. He leaned in to talk in a lower voice. "You're really cute, you know? What are you into? What do you like?" He ran his hand over Rick's chest, pausing to tweak his nipple through the thin cotton of his T-shirt. Rick bit his lip. He loved it when a guy played with his nipples.

Oli grinned. "Oh, you like that, don't you?"

"I'd say that's a big yes." A deep voice, rich with Antipodean tones, rumbled out, and Rick managed to drag his attention away from Oli's nipple play to look at Ben. Dark, brown eyes regarded him, matched with a sexy smile. "Hi there."

"Hi." It was all Rick could get out before his mouth was taken in a slow kiss, Ben's tongue teasing his lips before parting them and plunging inside. Rick moaned into Ben's mouth, surrendering completely as he reached for Ben to tug him closer. He was dimly aware of Oli pulling away, but stiffened when his dick was squeezed through his jeans.

"Oh, nice," Oli murmured and Rick gasped into Ben's passionate kiss when he felt Oli slip under the table in front of them, open his jeans and pull out his hardening cock. Rick tore himself away from Ben's assault on his lips to watch as Oli pushed Rick's knees apart and knelt between them, licking around the head of his cock before sucking him deep.

"Oh fucking hell." Rick was drowning in sensation. Ben's hands were all over him, stroking, teasing. Oli's hot, wet mouth encased his now solid dick, his tongue rolling over the flared head and flicking the underside, sending shivers through him. Ben's lips were on his neck, sucking up a storm, the feeling just the right side of painful. Rick grabbed the edge of the table and held on, striving not to get swept away by the rising tide of lust which engulfed him. Oli's head bobbed on his cock, narrowly missing the table top.

"Let's get out of here and go back to our place," Ben murmured into his ear. "Somewhere we can fuck for as long as we want."

"God, yes." The words rolled out of Rick's mouth instantly. He could feel Ben smiling against his neck. He glanced down to see Oli slowly licking up the stony length of his cock before pulling away to grin up at him as he tucked him back into his jeans. Rick was so hard he ached, and getting his dick to play along was no mean feat. Oli eased out from under the table and got to his feet, grasping Rick's hand and tugging him upright.

"What are we waitin' for?" That wicked grin of Oli's made all the muscles in Rick's abs quiver. As Rick was ushered out of the club, Ben leading the way, it occurred to him that allowing his cock to do his thinking might not be such a good idea. Then he took a long, good, hard look at the two sexy men who simply vibrated with sexual energy.

Fuck it.

Rick fucking loved this. His dick was buried deep in Oli's arse, his arms hooked under Oli's knees. Oli's long, slender cock rubbed against his abs. Oli pushed his head back into the pillow, the cords on his neck standing out as Rick plunged into him, filling him as each thrust of Ben's thick shaft filled Rick from behind.

"God, you have a tight arse," Ben grunted out. Rick shuddered when Ben's dick grazed his prostate, and then cried out as Ben bit into the soft tendons of his neck. Being bitten during sex always drove him crazy. And these two had wasted no time working out his hot buttons.

"I fucking love your big cock," Oli gasped out, his words punctuated by each thrust of Rick into his tight channel. Ben's firm hands gripped Oli's hips, connecting all three of them. Oli's gaze met Ben's over Rick's shoulder. "I want Rick to ride me, babe." He grinned, panting as Rick fucked him hard. Oli stared up at Rick. "You like that idea?"

Rick fucking *loved* that idea. "Oh God, yes."

Ben was out of him in seconds and helping him to straddle Oli, holding that long cock ready for Rick as he unrolled a condom down its stony length. Rick's mouth fused with Oli's and they kissed, all teeth and tongues, Rick breathing heavily, anxiously awaiting Oli's dick inside him. Ben had left him aching and wanting. But then Ben was there, pushing Oli's shaft against his hole, guiding it home. Rick sank down, feeling the rigid length fill him completely. He gasped as Ben spread his cheeks wide and Oli thrust up into him, hard and fast. He shivered as Oli nudged his spot with every single thrust.

"Oh fuck." The groan rolled out of him. Oli really knew what he was doing.

Ben's breath was warm on his neck. "Ever taken two dicks before, Rick?"

Rick felt Ben's finger ease into his hole, alongside Oli's shaft. *Oh hell.* "N-no," he gasped, as one finger suddenly became two. Rick was feeling very full. *Oh my fucking God...* Rick shuddered.

"Want to?" Ben whispered, his breath now hot against Rick's ear.

Rick trembled in anticipation. It was something he'd seen done once in a club and lots of times on his laptop, and he'd always wondered how it would feel. *Well, now's your chance...* "Y-yes," he whispered back.

Ben apparently needed no second invitation. Oli pulled him down to lie on his chest and Rick froze as Ben pressed his dick insistently against his hole, Rick's body resisting him. Rick gasped as Ben's insistence paid off: his entrance suddenly gave way as the head of Ben's cock slid into him, and all three men groaned.

"Oh FUCK!" Rick cried out. He'd never felt so stretched and full. He couldn't breathe as Ben pushed gently into him, his dick sliding alongside Oli's.

"How does it feel?" Ben asked.

Rick shuddered. "Oh God... s-so full," he cried out, his breathing ragged. "Fuck, I can feel both of you."

Oli lay moaning softly beneath him, his hands stroking Rick's back as he kissed his neck, his cock moving slowly inside Rick. Ben locked his arms, holding himself above Rick as he began to thrust, carefully at first, but gaining in momentum as his dick rocked into Rick at a powerful pace. Between the two of them, he and Oli quickly established a rhythm, one withdrawing as the other pushed into him.

"Oh fucking hell!" Rick gasped. "I can't ...tell you ...how that feels!" He panted with the effort, unable to hold back the constant moans of ecstasy as the two men fucked him, the pace increasing steadily.

Oli wrapped his hand wrapped around Rick's cock which jutted out at right angles from his body.

"Oh, fuck, yes!" Rick groaned.

Ben brought his mouth close to Rick's ear.

"You're so close, aren't you, baby?" Rick moaned, and Ben chuckled. "It feels so good, doesn't it? Being fucked by two guys, two hard cocks sliding into your willing arse." Ben's breathing was uneven. "That's it, Rick, let go, just let go..."

Rick suddenly cried out as a hard thrust of Oli's dick momentarily rendered him insensible, sending shock waves of pleasure to every nerve in his body. He felt the impending arrival of his orgasm, felt himself being pushed relentlessly towards the brink of ecstasy, and he simply let go, feeling the long waves of his climax roll over him, shattering him.

"Oh *fuuuuuuuck*!" Rick came, harder than he had ever come in his life, his anal muscles tightening around the two cocks which fucked him with abandon. His dick throbbed as his balls emptied hot come over Oli's fist, and he cried out again when muted heat filled him as both Oli and then Ben succumbed to their mutual orgasms.

"Oh hell," Ben cried out hoarsely, filling the condom with his seed, Oli groaning loudly beneath Rick, thrusting up as far into Rick's channel as he could, pumping hot come into his heat.

Rick sobbed incoherently as his orgasm racked

his body. Sandwiched between the two perspiring men, he collapsed, exhausted and shaken, as both spent cocks eased out of him. Ben and Oli stroked him, kissed him and each other, and he was grateful for their attention. The experience had left him weak and trembling, but what surprised him was the vague feeling of something stirring uneasily in his brain.

Is this it? Is this what my life is going to become?

Rick had no idea where that came from. He only knew that in that moment, he wanted more from life. Certainly more than hot encounters with guys who were virtually strangers to him.

As Ben and Oli tugged him toward their bathroom to shower, one thought plagued him over and over again, until it burned into his brain.

I want someone to love me.

Chapter Two

Saturday morning found Rick awake early, with a dry mouth, sandwiched between two gorgeous men, an unfamiliar sensation in the pit of his stomach—and a *very* sore arse. He blinked in the morning light which filtered through the blinds. Ben and Oli were still sound asleep, and getting out of bed to get to the bathroom without waking them was tricky, but he made it. The evidence of their night together lay on the rug beside the bed, in the form of several used condoms. The sight made him cringe. He'd never felt as big a slut as he did that morning, and each step made him wince, reinforcing the feeling. He grabbed his clothes from the floor where they'd been dropped in the heat of their encounter, went into the bathroom and shut the door quietly behind him.

Once inside he put his clothes over the side of the tub and stood in front of the washbasin, gripping the cool porcelain as he stared at his reflection in the mirror above it.

What the fuck were you doing? he asked himself. Okay, so it had been a night of firsts. His first threesome, first experience of double penetration—and definitely the first time he'd ever had the guilts over a night of hot sex. *So what's changed?* He didn't have a clue, but something had shifted in that brain of his. All he knew was that he wanted out of there. He managed a quick wash and then got dressed, everything done as quietly as possible. He didn't want his hosts to awaken. As he made his way through their apartment, he got his first real glimpse of it. The night before, he'd been lost in a fog of lust. When he quietly slipped out their front door and onto the street, it suddenly occurred to him that he didn't have a clue where he was. He shivered in the cold morning air. But once he'd found the nearest tube station and realized he was in Clapham, it wasn't long before he was on his way back to his little flat.

He wasn't sure what he did for the rest of the weekend. He seemed to be functioning on autopilot. Inside his head was a real mess. He went through the motions, food shopping, cleaning, watching a little TV, and all the while his brain wouldn't stop. He got very little sleep, that much he did recall, and by the time Monday morning rolled around again, he arrived at Trinity's building feeling exhausted and looking every inch of it. Blake had already put on the coffee and he poured himself a big mug. The way he was feeling, he was going to need it fed to him intravenously. He went back to his office, not really wanting to talk to Blake or Ed, who were usually the first ones to arrive. It was bad enough that he'd have the morning team meeting to attend. He was in no mood to talk to anyone.

Rick sat at his desk, gazing out over the London skyline. Normally he loved his view. He'd moved to London with his family at the age of fifteen when Dad got a new job, and he'd been so excited to be living in such a huge city after the peace and quiet of Kent. And when he finally moved into his own place six years ago, it felt so liberating to have all of London on his doorstep. Shops, nightclubs, theatres…. Right now? He just wanted to crawl under his duvet and leave all of London outside his front door.

His performance during the team meeting must

have been worthy of an Oscar, because no one noticed that he wasn't his usual effervescent self. Well, he *thought* it had been, until Will appeared at his office about half an hour later, leaning nonchalantly against the door frame and carrying two mugs of coffee precariously in one hand and a couple of chocolate muffins in the other. Rick should have sent him packing there and then with some excuse or other, but the sight of chocolate muffins was too much. At least, that was what he told himself later to account for his momentary weakness.

Will grinned when Rick waved him in with a resigned huff. "See, I thought you might not want to talk, so I brought reinforcements." He waved the muffins. "You are *so* easy."

"Shut up, hand it over and I *might* promise not to hurt you," Rick growled.

Will tossed him the muffins and then placed the mugs on the desk. He went back to the door and pushed it shut. Rick watched him warily. By the time Will had dragged the comfy but worn armchair from its position against the wall to the front of his desk and then flopped into it, all trace of humour had gone. He regarded Rick steadily, his eyes full of concern. "So, you going to tell me what's going on?"

Rick gave as innocent a look as he could muster. "Don't know what you're talking about," he said lightly, opening the cellophane to get to the chocolatey goodness that called to him. He took a big bite and sagged into his seat. *God, thank you for chocolate.*

"Sorry, but I'm not buying it," Will said. "I *know* you, cutie, remember? So out with it." His gaze narrowed. "Okay, what did you do?"

Rick's mouth fell open. "What makes you think

I did something?"

Will snorted. "I refer you to my previous statement." He picked up his mug and took a long drink. Lowering it, he gave Rick a hard stare. Rick squirmed and Will's expression softened. "Look, I know there's something wrong. And you'll feel much better if you tell me, honest."

Rick stared into his coffee. The daft thing was, he knew Will was right. "All right," he began reluctantly, and he proceeded to tell Will about his Friday night adventure, as he put it. He fully expected Will to give him an expression of shock and mock outrage, and then ask for more juicy details. What he wasn't prepared for, was Will's dawning look of horror.

"Oh God, Rick, you didn't. *Tell* me you didn't."

Rick frowned. "Well, I didn't think it warranted *that* extreme a reaction."

Will shook his head. "You don't get it. I *know* Ben and Oli. And okay, they're nice blokes socially, good mates even, but *Christ*, Rick, you're playing with fire there." He gazed earnestly at Rick. "I've seen how they play. I mean——"

"Okay, you need to stop right there, all right?"

Will's mouth snapped shut instantly. The look of surprise on his face was almost comic.

Rick nodded in satisfaction. "Better." He took a slurp of his coffee and another bite of muffin, then he leaned back into his chair. "I've done a lot of thinking ever since I woke up on Saturday morning. I took a long, hard look at myself, and I'll be honest, I didn't like what I saw."

Will nodded, his face solemn.

Rick inhaled slowly. "Don't get me wrong. The

sex was hot, and those two… Yeah, I've never had a night like it. But when you come down to it, that's all it was. Just hot sex. And then I started thinking. Fuck, I haven't *stopped* thinking about it all weekend. I don't want to do this anymore. I don't want to have a succession of one-night stands, quick fucks in bathrooms, casual sex with guys who I'll probably never see again. I'm sorry, but I want more. I want to *connect* with someone. I want something permanent. I'm twenty-eight, and there has to be more to my fucking life than this." His voice quavered.

Will grasped his hand. He said nothing, but his eyes were full of pain.

Rick gave him a weak smile. "God, what do I sound like?" Will's hand tightened around his.

"Like someone who's making a lot of sense," Will said softly. "And whatever you decide, I'm right behind you, okay? If you need someone to talk to, vent at, share with… I'm your man."

Rick gave him a grateful smile, and then frowned as Will's expression morphed into something decidedly more pensive. "What is it?"

Will sighed. "Blake and I had a long talk over the weekend. He wants me to quit my job as his PA— and I've agreed."

"What?" Rick gaped. "But… but you love this job!" Will nodded. "What did he say, exactly?"

Will cocked his head. "Did you ever read that book Blake gave to Beth to edit? Out in the Cold?" Rick became still. "You did, didn't you? I thought only Beth and Peter saw it."

Rick gave him a sheepish glance. "Beth emailed me a copy once she'd edited it. Said it was absolutely brilliant, and how she hoped Blake would bring the author over to Trinity." He squinted at Will. "What about it?"

Will took a deep breath. "What I'm about to tell you doesn't go outside this room, okay?"

Rick nodded quickly. "You have my word, mate."

Will stared at his coffee mug for a moment and then met Rick's intent gaze. "I wrote it."

Rick's jaw dropped. "Wow. I am seriously impressed. It was such a great book." Rick hadn't been able to put it down. The book had made him laugh, smile, but he'd also cried at the events of the young rent boy's life. "What gave you the idea?"

Will's gaze was troubled. "Terry was me, Rick."

For a long moment, Rick couldn't say a word. His throat constricted. And then he looked at Will's earnest face, saw the anxiety plainly written there. Rick was out of his chair in a flash. He went around his desk and pulled Will up out of his seat into a fierce hug, hearing him gasp as the unexpectedness of Rick's embrace knocked the stuffing out of him.

"Bloody hell, Will," Rick said into his ear, his arms tight around Will's lean body. Will trembled. "Oh God, mate. Your life was just…" Words failed him.

They stood like that for a moment or two, until Will broke free and stepped back, wiping his eyes with the back of his hand. Rick gave a weak grin, doing the same thing.

"God, what a pair, eh?"

Will sniffed and smiled as he sat back down, reaching for his coffee. Rick copied him.

Rick eyed him keenly. "So is Blake going to publish it?"

Will shook his head. "I told him no. It's too

personal. And besides, it only takes one smart bastard to read it and start looking up stuff about my past. I couldn't cope with that."

Rick leaned back into his chair. "So what *did* Blake say?"

Will's face was suddenly a mask. "He told me to do something else with my life, namely, write, and that he'd support me in every way he could while I write."

Rick sat upright. "What's wrong?" When Will arched his eyebrows, Rick snorted. "You said you know me? Well, guess what, mate—it works both ways. What else did the pair of you say that you're not telling me?"

Will huffed. "You read the book, so you know about the debts I ran up with my studies." Rick nodded. "Blake offered to pay off my debts, but I told him a flat no. If I did that, it.... Let's just say, it felt wrong. I told him I wanted to pay them off myself, *my* way."

Rick thought for a moment. If the book was truly autobiographical, then Will had started work as an escort. "Have you kicked the escort agency into touch?" Rick blurted out.

Will became still, regarding him in silence, and then he nodded. "I told Jenny—she runs J's—that I would no longer be working for her. Not that I'd done a single job for months. Not since I met Blake." He gave a half smile. "Blake thinks I'm showing incredible strength of character. I told him I was just being me. I couldn't be any other way."

Rick regarded his friend warmly. "You're really going to leave Trinity?"

Will nodded. "I handed in my resignation this morning. I leave in ten weeks' time."

Rick sighed heavily. "So no sooner do I get used to you being around, you're going to up and leave."

Will got up from his chair and came around to Rick's side of the desk. He took hold of Rick's hand. "Just because I'm going to leave here, doesn't mean you and I are going to lose touch. Not if I can help it." He gazed intently at Rick. "I'm not about to lose my friend."

The tight fist around Rick's heart eased. "Glad to hear it." He grinned up at Will. "Then you'd better piss off and let me work, or Blake will have you out of here even faster for distracting his staff."

Will relinquished his hand and got up. "And on that note…" He walked to the door and turned before exiting. His face was solemn. "Thanks, Rick."

Rick knew it was an unspoken plea. "I won't say a word, I promise."

Will's expression of gratitude said more than words. Rick stared at his monitor for a moment, thinking about Will's revelation. If the book was anything to go by, Will had a great career as a writer ahead of him. Despite Will's reassurances that they wouldn't lose touch, it saddened Rick to think of Trinity without him. He'd come to love having Will around.

At least I haven't lost him as a friend.

Friday night came and went, with Rick deciding to stay home. He watched TV, ate a takeaway pizza and generally vegged out. But by the time Saturday night came, he was overtaken by the urge to go dancing. And that meant only one place—Heaven.

He loved going to Heaven. As gay clubs went, it was great. What Rick loved was the combination of music that seemed to pulse right through him, and hot guys out to enjoy themselves, dancing 'til dawn.

Not to mention the number of times I hooked up in dark corners.

Rick tried not to think about that. *I'm going there to dance 'til I'm dead on my feet. And if someone chats me up, then I'll enjoy it. It'll be a bonus.*

He wasn't expecting someone to sweep him off his feet, but he couldn't deny the hope was there. *Just as long as the night doesn't end with me in someone's bed—or him in mine.*

Rick had meant every word he'd uttered.

Heaven was exactly what the doctor ordered. Rick had spent a good three hours letting the music lead him as he swayed on the dance floor. Now and again he cast admiring glances at some of the gorgeous guys who surrounded him, but mostly he tuned out the world and lost himself on some beautiful plateau where music thrummed through him. He felt vibrant, alive—and observed.

It was gone midnight when Rick first spotted him. He became aware of a pair of blue eyes, set in a pale face, framed by long, blond hair. The guy was tall, and definitely verging on being a gym bunny, judging by the abs that were visible through his black, mesh shirt. Not to mention those strong-looking arms. But definitely worth a second—or even third—view.

Who am I kidding? The guy's just… beautiful. It was the only word that did him justice.

Rick stopped to drink down a bottle of water, still conscious of being watched. He stood with his back to the bar, trying not to stare. Mr. Beautiful hadn't made a move, and that careful scrutiny was beginning to creep Rick out. He deliberated marching over to the table where the guy sat, and demanding to ask what it was about Rick that was so interesting, when Mr. Beautiful finally made a move. He rose and walked slowly toward Rick.

God, he even moves *beautifully.*

When he reached Rick, he stopped and leaned against the bar, mimicking Rick's stance. He inclined his head and gave a slow, totally captivating, sexy smile.

"Can I buy you a drink?" His voice was low, but it carried about the music.

Rick held up his water. "Thanks, but I'm fine."

The guy nodded. "I saw you drinking, but I figured it was about time I said something." The sexy smile turned a little sheepish. "I haven't been able to take my eyes off you."

Rick chuckled. "I did notice. I mean, it's not as if you were subtle about it."

Mr. Beautiful bit his lip, and Rick caught his breath. It was adorable to watch this Adonis become flustered. "Yeah, sorry about that."

Rick turned to give the guy his full attention. "Hey, don't apologize." He smiled. "It isn't every night I find some beautiful creature watching my every move." He winked. "Although I was beginning to worry that I had a stalker." He extended a hand. "I'm Rick, by the way."

His stalker took his hand and shook it firmly. He had quite a grip. "Julian." He cocked his head. "Sure I can't get you a drink?"

Rick shook his head as he drained the bottle of its last drops. "I'm sure." He was always wary of guys buying him drinks. Too many horror stories abounded of date rape drugs. His heart pounded as he plucked up courage. "But… how about joining me on the dance floor?"

Julian grinned. "Love to."

Rick grasped Julian's hand and led him out onto the floor, where lithe bodies undulated to a slow number with a heady bass. He expected Julian to press up close against him, but when his dance partner kept to a respectful distance, Rick found his heart pounding all the more. Gorgeous *and* considerate? *Oh, this one has promise.*

They danced together for maybe half an hour, before Julian motioned that he wanted a drink. Rick nodded and followed him back to the bar. When Julian asked if he wanted anything, Rick broke his rule and asked for a Coke. When the barman placed the opened bottle in front of him, Julian picked it up and handed it to Rick.

"Keep your thumb over it. You never know who might drop something in there these days." His gaze was serious.

Rick nodded numbly. *Okay, so where has this guy been hiding all my life?* Julian was certainly creating a very favourable impression. And when they'd spent the next hour chatting over the music about favorite bands, films and TV shows, and Julian still hadn't made a move on him, Rick was even more impressed. Julian listened attentively and asked intelligent questions. He soon got an idea of Rick's dry sense of humour and had him in stitches. It was a total shock when the DJ announced the last track, and Rick realized the club was about to close. He'd been oblivious to the passage of time.

Wow. I think I may finally have hit the jackpot—a genuinely nice guy. The thought filled Rick with hope. And just like that, he knew he wanted to see more of Julian. *Not going to let this one get away.*

"Angelo Tarallo, you haven't taken your eyes off that bloke all night."

Angelo pulled himself back into the moment. His friend Len regarded him with amusement. Angelo gave an embarrassed laugh.

"Sorry, Len. Yeah, I spotted him earlier when he arrived." He and Len had only been in Heaven for about half an hour when he'd spotted the guy. Len had gone off to dance with some little twink, leaving Angelo alone to admire the scenery.

"Your type?" his mate asked with a smirk. Angelo merely grinned. Len knew him too well. The minute he'd laid eyes on the tousled-haired young man with the big blue eyes, Angelo was smitten. *My type? Baby, you're my dream guy.* The way he danced, oblivious to the stares of the men around him, totally unaware of just how hot he was. He was a couple of inches shorter than Angelo, he estimated, with a slim body that moved sinuously to the rhythms which seemed to flow around and through him.

"Definitely my type," Angelo murmured. He'd tried not to make his scrutiny obvious. The last thing he wanted was to freak the guy out, making him think he had a stalker. Angelo had been dying to walk over there and start up a conversation. About what, he hadn't decided. But it became a moot point when someone else got there first.

And that was when Angelo started watching for an entirely different reason.

His heart sank when he recognized Julian Emerson. *Oh fuck.* Of all the men to take an interest in Angelo's dream guy, why the hell did it have to be Julian? The man was Bad News. Of course, all Angelo had to go on were rumours, but if *half* of them were true, his dream guy could be in trouble if he stayed around Julian for very long. And as the music throbbed on into the early hours, Angelo couldn't stop watching the pair. Despite his efforts not to make it obvious, Len's comment told him he'd failed miserably.

Angelo watched as his dream guy and Julian got into a clinch. His chest tightened as they kissed. It was clearly nothing too heavy, but Angelo held his breath, watching anxiously. When they broke apart and said their goodbyes, Angelo heaved a huge sigh of relief when they didn't leave together. *That's it, baby,* Angelo silently told him. *Don't you go home with him.* He followed Dream Guy's exit from the club and then his eyes narrowed as he regarded Julian. Angelo was at Heaven every Friday and Saturday night, and from what he'd observed, so was Julian.

I'm going to make sure I'm here every weekend from now on, he thought grimly, his gaze fixed on Julian. *Because if that gorgeous guy comes back, I'll be watching you like a hawk.*

Someone had to, for his Dream Guy's sake.

Chapter Three

Rick poured himself a cup of coffee and then reached into the fridge for his lunch, a plastic container filled with pasta he'd made on Sunday. As he emptied the box onto a plate to place it in the microwave, he whistled to himself.

What a difference a week makes, eh?

He couldn't stop thinking about Saturday night. He'd had such a good time. The dancing had been fun, but Julian had been the icing on the cake. The guy had been so attentive, so considerate. *I've waited such a long time to meet someone like him*, Rick thought as he watched the pasta revolving slowly in the microwave. All night he'd kept waiting for the other shoe to fall, but Julian hadn't made a single wrong move. When he'd asked to kiss Rick goodnight, Rick had expected him to take things further, but the gentle but thorough kiss had taken his breath away.

And boy, can he kiss.

Rick was astounded to find his pulse racing at the mere memory of those warm lips on his. *If that's what his kiss does....* Rick shivered.

"Oh, I'm dying to ask what you were thinking about just then."

Lizzie stood by the door, arms folded, eyes bright with amusement.

Rick shook himself. He hadn't even noticed her enter the kitchen. "None of your business," he said with a wink, tapping the side of his nose.

Lizzie giggled. "Aw, spoilsport." She grinned.

"I'll tell if you will."

The microwave pinged and Rick carefully removed the plate of hot pasta and cheese sauce. He sniffed the air, his stomach rumbling as he took a seat at the small table and then reached behind him into the drawer of the cabinet for a fork. He gazed at Lizzie with interest. Her cheeks were bright pink. "Oh? And what have you got to tell?"

Lizzie took the seat facing him. "Okay, I've got to tell someone." She bit her lip. "I've got a date." The pink tinge to her cheeks deepened.

Rick arched his eyebrows. "Oh really?" He'd known Lizzie for five years. The Belgian head of the translation department hadn't had a lot of luck where men were concerned. She often regaled him with tales of her disastrous dates, ending up with both of them laughing. "Let's hope this one is better than the last one. Remind me. What did he want to talk about all evening?" Rick smirked. As if he needed reminding.

Lizzie gave a low growl that took him by surprise. "Oh yes, joke about it, why don't you? You weren't the one who had to sit through dinner while your date described his haemorrhoids and what he was doing to treat them—in *great* detail, I might add."

Rick guffawed. "Oh yeah, I'd forgotten." Lizzie squinted at him and he snickered. "Aw, come on, you have to admit, it *was* funny." Her arms tightened across her chest. Rick hurried to placate her. "Okay, so tell me about this date. Is he nice? Where'd you meet him?"

Lizzie's eyes sparkled. "Here."

Rick frowned. "What? Is he an author or something?" He couldn't recollect seeing anyone recently.

Lizzie smiled. "He was at the New Year's Eve party. Blake's friend, Dave, the photographer."

"Oh!" Rick grinned. Now that she mentioned it, Rick recalled seeing the two chatting up a storm in a corner of the conference room. "So when did he ask you out?"

Lizzie sighed happily. "He asked for my number as he left the party. I didn't really think I'd hear from him again. I thought he was just being polite. But he rang me last night." She hugged herself. "He told me it had taken him this long to get up the courage to ask me out."

Rick liked the sound of Dave. He'd seemed like an decent bloke, and if Blake trusted him, that was good enough. Rick was fond of Lizzie. In fact, he was fond of all of Blake's team, but he had a soft spot for the quietly-spoken lady who always had a smile and a kind word for him.

"So where is he taking you?"

Lizzie lowered her voice. "He's making me dinner—at his apartment." Her cheeks heated up.

Rick gaped in mock horror. "Why, Lizzie Jordan, you little hussy."

Lizzie straightened. "It's just dinner," she insisted. She speared him with a look. "All right, I shared. Your turn."

Rick smiled. "Nothing to tell as yet. I…I met someone on Saturday night at a club, that's all."

"Yeah, but what *we're* all dying to know, is did you leave him there—or did he get to see the inside of your bachelor pad?" Will asked with a smirk as he entered the kitchen, Blake behind him. Will went over to the coffee machine and poured out two mugs.

Blake chuckled. "Well, aren't you going to tell

us?"

Will chimed in. "Yeah, give us details, we demand details!"

Rick lifted his chin and looked Blake in the eye. "If you must pry, I left the club alone." He shrugged, as if this was a perfectly normal state of affairs.

Blake whistled and Will smiled widely. "I was convinced you'd had a wonderfully dirty weekend, judging by all the smiles I've seen since you got here this morning," Blake admitted.

Rick's phone chimed, and he took it from his pocket, trying not to sigh with relief. *Talk about being saved by the bell.* He knew Will would be by later, demanding to know more, but Rick didn't want to discuss it. It was as if he felt the mere act of talking about Julian would somehow jinx it.

He opened up the incoming text and then caught his breath.

Would you like to go for a meal with me on Wednesday night? Julian X

Rick stared at the words on the screen. They'd exchanged numbers, but Rick hadn't expected to hear from him so soon. His heartbeat raced at the idea of seeing Julian again.

"Rick? Earth to Rick, come in, Rick!"

Rick realized he'd zoned out. The three people in the small kitchen all regarded him with amusement. Will was grinning like a lunatic. "Okay, where did *you* just go?"

"Tell you later," Rick said with an equally wide grin, pocketing his phone. He hadn't replied yet, but there was no way he was going to stand there with Will watching while he typed an answer.

And besides, do you know what your answer will be?

Oh, that part was easy. Yes. In a heartbeat.

Rick looked around the restaurant and smiled. "I couldn't believe it when you suggested having dinner at a restaurant called the Gay Hussar. And in Soho, no less."

Julian returned his smile. "Yeah, the name—and the area—conjure up all kinds of images, don't they?"

Rick nodded. And none of them matched what he was seeing. A long dining room, complete with one wall filled with mirrors, the other with sketches of famous people who'd dined there. At one end, there were bookcases from floor to ceiling. Even the ceiling was impressive, with ornate mouldings. The tables were laid out in two rows, one side having plush, padded benches. "It's a beautiful place. What's the food like? I've never tried Hungarian food before."

Julian's eyes glittered. "Delicious. Wait and see."

When the waiter brought their menus, Rick looked with interest to see what was on offer. It was enough to make his mouth water. "Oh God. I'm *soooo* going to be spoilt for choice here." It took several minutes before he arrived at a decision, but eventually he decided on a starter of fish dumplings in a creamy dill and mushroom sauce with rice, to be followed by a veal goulash pancake with spinach. There was no way he was about to *try* pronouncing the Hungarian names of the dishes, so he resorted to pointing politely. The waiter didn't seem to mind. Julian was more adventurous in his choices. He chose the chilled wild cherry soup to start with, followed by duck livers sautéed with onions, bacon and paprika.

Rick was relieved when Julian chose the wine. It wasn't something he knew much about, and he was impressed when the bottle of Tokaji Muscat Blanc arrived. The medium white wine had a smooth finish and was very drinkable.

Julian raised his glass in a toast. "To a delightful evening, with even more delightful company."

Rick's cheeks grew hot. He'd never been taken to dinner on a date before, at least, not in so elegant a setting. He glanced along the wall as they awaited their starters. "There seem to have been lots of politicians eating here." An impressive amount, judging by the number of famous faces which stared back at him.

Julian nodded. "This place is famous. I admit it. I was trying to impress you." His face flushed. Rick thought it was adorable. Julian wore a black shirt, open at the collar, with a black jacket and black pants. His long hair was pulled back and held in a long clip. The overall image was that of a very sexy man.

"Then you succeeded," Rick replied softly. Julian's eyes glowed.

The food was excellent. Rick took it slowly, savouring both the rich flavours and the wonderful setting. As first dates went, it was certainly a success. As they ate, Julian asked questions about Rick. He told Julian about his parents and his sister, Maggie, and Rick's childhood in Kent. Julian told him about his job as a commodities broker in the City, which sounded exciting. He asked about Rick's work at Trinity. One hour became two, and by the time coffee arrived, Rick was so relaxed he'd almost melted into his seat. Julian had been the perfect dinner date, and there definitely been a romantic feel to the whole evening. Rick had expected him to split the bill, but was surprised when Julian told him politely but firmly that dinner was on him.

As they exited the restaurant, Rick let out a contented sigh.

Julian smiled. "You had a good time tonight, didn't you?"

Rick nodded, not bothering to hide his grin. "I had a *wonderful* time."

Julian seemed delighted. "Then how about I find us a taxi and get you home? I realize it's a work night."

Rick did his best to mask his surprise. *This keeps getting better and better.* "Thank you," he said sincerely. Julian said nothing but began to look up and down the street for a black cab. Rick couldn't stop smiling. He was sure the cab driver must have thought he was nuts, every time he looked in the mirror on the short journey to Southwark and saw this guy grinning away to himself like a lunatic. Julian sat beside him, their hands clasped together on Julian's knee, and every now and then he glanced at Rick and smiled.

When the cab pulled up outside the block of flats where Rick lived, Julian got out with him, having told the driver to wait. He walked Rick up to the main front door and then cupped his face, pulling him into a soft kiss, that quickly progressed until Rick was gasping for breath, his arms reaching around to grab hold of Julian and cling tightly to him. Julian slipped an arm under Rick's jacket and around his waist, pressing Rick against him. The warm, heady scent of Julian's cologne enticed his senses.

"Let me stay the night?" Julian whispered into Rick's ear, and then he kissed his neck, moving lower to where Rick's heartbeat pulsed, nuzzling the skin.

Rick stiffened. *Oh fuck. Damn. I knew it was too*

good to last.

"Julian," he began, his voice cracking as Julian sucked at his neck, before slowly tracing a line up to Rick's earlobe with his tongue. *How in hell am I supposed to concentrate when he does that?* "Julian." He tried again. "Please, wait."

Something in his voice must have cut through the fog of lust. Julian stopped, pulled away and looked at Rick, head tilted. "Is there something wrong?"

Rick drew in several deep, calming breaths before speaking. There was no denying it, Julian turned him on. But Rick was determined to stand by his decision, even if his body cried out for more.

"Julian, I'm sorry, but would you understand if I said I didn't want to do this after only one date?" Inside his head he prayed furiously that Julian wouldn't let him down, wouldn't step down from the pedestal that Rick had placed him upon.

Julian stared at him for a second, his expression perplexed. Then his face straightened. "You're serious."

Rick nodded, his eyes never leaving Julian's face.

Julian regarded him steadily, his face unreadable. He sighed. "Okay. If that's what you want."

Okay, it was the result I wanted, but not exactly delivered the way I wanted it.

"You're really okay with this?" Rick pressed.

Julian gave a short nod. "I said so, didn't I?" He gave Rick a smile that didn't quite reach his eyes. Then he seemed to relent. His expression softened. "Yeah, it's fine, baby." He leaned forward and planted a chaste kiss on Rick's forehead. "Now get in there and get some sleep. I wouldn't want you tired at work tomorrow because of me."

And with that he turned and walked back to the waiting taxi, pausing once to wave at Rick before climbing in. Rick watched as the taxi pulled away from the curb.

Okay, you got what you wanted. Satisfied?

He'd gotten what he wanted, all right. The trouble was, at this moment, it wasn't making him happy.

You'll feel better about this tomorrow, he told himself. *Yeah. Maybe.*

"So you had fun, right?" Will pressed. "It was a good date?"

"Yes," insisted Rick for what must have been the umpteenth time. "For God's sake, Will, you're worse than my mother. Even *she* doesn't hassle me *this* much after a date." He hadn't told Will about Julian's final request of the evening, but he knew it was only a matter of time before Will wormed it out of him.

"And he didn't try it on?" Will pried. He took a bite of his cheese sandwich and squinted at him. "Come one, cutie, there's something you're not telling me."

Rick put his empty coffee mug down onto the kitchen work top with a bang. "Okay, if it makes you happy? He wanted to spend the night, but I told him no." He stared resolutely at Will. "See? I meant what I said, Will. No more diving into bed with guys at the first available opportunity." He ran his fingers through his tousled mop of hair, knowing he was only making it look worse, but right then and there, he couldn't give a shit. He'd done the right thing, damn it.

So why did you have such a restless night? He couldn't get over Julian's initial reaction. Had he imagined it? Okay, so Julian had said it was fine. *Then why am I not convinced?*

"What's the matter?" Will's voice was soft.

"I don't know!" Rick wailed. "It was such a great night, then he went and asked…. And that look on his face… Oh shit, Will, he's just so…." He broke off, unable to frame with words what was going on in his head.

Will regarded him in silence, lips pursed. Rick knew that look. Will was up to something.

"I have an idea," he said at last.

Rick arched his eyebrows. "Oh, I can't wait to hear this."

Will simply waited until Rick had straightened his face. "I think I should meet this Julian."

Rick guffawed. "Er, since when do you vet my boyfriends?" He rolled his eyes. "I swear, you *are* worse than my mother." He let out a dry chuckle.

Will shook his head. "No, listen. This guy obviously impressed you. Otherwise you wouldn't be so upset by his reaction. And you plainly want things to progress with him. So… how about you and Julian go on a double date with me and Blake?"

Rick just stared. "You're serious."

Will nodded. "Let us check him out. Give you our honest opinion. Because that's what this is all about, right? The way he reacted has given you some doubts about Mr. Perfect."

Rick scowled. "Don't call him that. Besides, I probably read too much into it. " Still, it couldn't hurt. He trusted Will and Blake. If Julian got their seal of approval, Rick would know it was just him being paranoid.

Will grinned. "You're thinking about it, aren't you?"

Rick squeezed Will with his eyeballs. "You know me far too well. It's scary sometimes how you seem to know what's going on in my head."

To his surprise, Will leaned across and kissed him on top of his head. "I just love you, mate, that's all. And I don't want you to be hurt. So if us meeting Julian puts your mind at rest, then all the better." Then his gaze narrowed. "But if he's not kosher, he'd better watch out. I look out for my friends, and if I think for a *second* that he might hurt you…." He let his words trail off, but the look in his eyes was enough.

Rick's chest tightened. Will was the best friend he'd ever had. "Thanks," he said quietly. "I'll ask him, okay? Once you've cleared it with your hubby-to-be, of course." He winked.

Will snorted. "Blake won't mind. You leave him to me." With one final grin, Will dropped his empty sandwich bag into the bin and left the kitchen.

Rick took out his phone and scrolled through to find Julian's number. He stared at it for a moment.

Go on, ask him. He can only say yes or no, can't he?

Rick sighed and clicked Call. It rang five times before Julian answered. There was the loud buzz of voices in the background.

"Rick! Hi." Julian sounded genuinely pleased to hear from him. "To what do I owe this pleasure?" He heard the scrape of chair legs on the floor. "Hang on, it's too bloody noisy in here, Give me a sec." There was a pause, and then the voices became muted. "That's better." Rick could hear him more clearly. "I didn't think I'd hear from you so soon."

"Yeah, well, I had an idea and I wanted to run it by you." Rick's heartbeat raced. "How would you feel about coming on a double date with me one night?"

A brief moment of silence. "Well, that depends." Rick could hear the cautious note in Julian's voice. "Double date with whom, exactly?"

"My boss Blake and his fiancé Will. I think I told you about them last night?" Rick waited anxiously.

"Yeah, I remember." Julian didn't sound particularly enthralled by the prospect.

"Look, if you don't want to, that's okay, really." Rick's heart sank.

Another pause. "No, that'll be cool. Why don't you arrange it with them and then let me know?"

"Sure, I'll do that." Rick waited to see if anything else was forthcoming, but the other end of the line was quiet. "Okay, I'll let you get back to work."

"Thanks, baby. I'm up against it right now. We'll talk more when you've sorted it, 'kay?" They exchanged goodbyes and then Julian disconnected the call.

Rick sat and stared at the screen. Maybe it was his imagination, but he got the distinct impression Julian was more than a little reluctant. Then he thought about it more carefully.

If he was that reluctant, he'd have refused, right? I mean, why would he say yes if he didn't want to go?

Rick didn't have an answer for that one.

Chapter Four

Rick loved the restaurant Blake chose for the date. The food was to die for. The setting was elegant, intimate...

So why aren't I having a good time?

Things had started off so well. Julian had met them all at the restaurant bar, where they'd had cocktails. The atmosphere had been relaxed, and Rick had finally got rid of the butterflies in his stomach that had plagued him for most of Saturday. There'd been a lot of small talk while they'd waited for their table, and he'd been relieved that the conversations had been lively.

So where did it start going wrong? Oh yeah—the menu.

Not that there was anything wrong with the menu. It was Julian's decision to order for *both* of them that had started off the butterflies again. Julian probably meant well, but Rick could tell by Will's arched eyebrows and Blake's narrowed gaze that they didn't like it. Rick didn't know what to think. Okay, so maybe Julian had really good taste, maybe he was something of a connoisseur, but Rick was perfectly capable of ordering his own dinner, thank you very much.

Then why didn't you speak up?

That was easy. Rick didn't want to rock the boat. And he wanted Julian to feel comfortable. So if that meant letting him choose their courses, Rick wasn't about to stop him. When the food arrived, Rick had to agree Julian had chosen well. The chicken was tender, flavoured beautifully with tarragon and sage and Julian seemed really pleased that he was enjoying it.

"See, I knew you'd like it," he declared, eyes gleaming. His hand stroked Rick's, a soft, intimate touch that made him shiver.

Rick didn't mind the touching: the restaurant seemed to be gay-friendly and no one batted an eyelid. But Julian kept *on* touching him, a pat on the arm here, a squeeze of the hand there, almost as if he couldn't leave Rick alone. And then there were Julian's tiny glances at Will while he was doing it, as if to make sure Will had noticed. Yeah, he'd noticed, all right. Rick could tell from the expression on Will's face that he wasn't happy.

Julian excused himself to go to the bathroom while they were waiting for the coffee to arrive, and Rick took advantage of his absence to speak to Will. He leaned across the table and lowered his voice.

"What's wrong?"

Will tightened his lips. "Don't tell me you think he's behaving normally?"

"Not here," Blake cautioned, laying his hand on Will's arm. His gaze met Rick's. "We can talk about this another time. He'll be back in a moment." He gave his fiancé a firm stare and Will huffed as he sat back in his chair.

The coffee arrived just before Julian returned to the table. He kissed Rick on top of his head as he sat down. "Did I miss anything?"

"Not a thing," Rick said. He took a sip of coffee and gave a sad smile. He raised his cup toward Blake. "They can't make coffee as good as yours, Blake."

Blake sighed dramatically. "It's a true gift, shared by only a few."

Rick snickered.

Julian stroked the back of his hand as it lay on the crisp, white tablecloth. "I'm sure your coffee is every bit as delicious as Blake's." He winked. "I'm hoping to sample some tonight."

Rick stiffened. Okay, so it was their second date, but he'd had no intention of asking Julian back to his flat. Will frowned.

Julian drank his coffee in silence, staring ahead at nothing in particular, his jaw tight.

Rick stirred a lump of sugar into his coffee, watching the dark liquid swirl. There was something tight around his chest, making it difficult to breathe. He liked Julian, he really did, but that didn't mean he was about to change his mind. *And if he's serious about getting to know me, then surely he'd respect my wishes.* He sighed internally. It was far easier when he just jumped into bed with a guy. *This is what I get for not wanting to be a slut,* he thought. *A stomach in knots and a gorgeous man who's probably going to dump me if he doesn't get what he wants.*

The meal over, Blake asked for the bill. When the waiter brought it to their table, Julian moved as if to take it, but Blake stopped him. "I insist on paying. It was our idea to ask you two along in the first place." When Julian pulled a face, he smiled politely. "Tell you what, you can pay next time, all right?"

Julian's returning smile was equally polite, but Rick saw the tension in his jaw.

As they walked out of the restaurant into the chill January night air, Will extended a hand to Julian. "It was great to meet you."

Julian shook it and smiled. Rick was getting used to seeing that particular smile. It was the one that didn't reach his eyes. "Yeah, same here. Rick has talked about you two so much, it was good to put faces to the names." He cast a glance in Rick's direction. "In fact, Will, he talked about *you* so much over dinner this week, I was beginning to wonder if I had a rival for his affections."

Rick froze. *What the hell?* For one, he didn't think he'd mentioned Will *that* much during their date, and two, how could Julian even *think* of saying such a thing in front of Blake?

Blake's eyes flashed. Those azure eyes were suddenly glacial. Will's expression was cold. He opened his mouth to speak but Blake caught his eye and shook his head. He speared Julian with a cool stare. "I'm sure after spending an evening with us, you've realized that there is absolutely nothing to your suspicions." He reached across the table and clasped Will's hand. "I'm glad Rick and Will have such a strong friendship."

Will gave Blake such a warm look of love that Rick's throat tightened.

Julian stiffened. "Of course. Me too." He turned to Rick with a smile. "So, going to invite me back to your place, gorgeous?"

Rick had had enough. "Actually, Julian, I was going to share a cab with Will and Blake. They live not far from me, and I know I'd be taking you out of your way." The evening had been a revelation, and right now, he wanted to think.

Julian's eyes widened. He clearly hadn't been expecting that. "I see. Well, in that case, I'll say thank you again for a pleasant evening, gentlemen." He gave Rick a peck on the cheek. "And I'll speak to you at some point, okay?" He flashed him a tight smile and then turned to walk briskly up the street, pulling his coat around him as protection from the wind, his long hair caught in a ponytail down his back. He didn't turn around.

Rick stared after him in consternation. *Oh fuck.*

Blake touched his elbow and leaned in close. "Since when do we live near you?"

Rick sighed heavily. "I couldn't think of anything else to say."

Will put his arm around Rick's shoulders. "Come on, let's get you home." He squeezed him lightly and Rick leaned into his friend. Blake had already flagged down a black cab. When they climbed inside, Will pulled Rick to sit between him and Blake.

"Tell me you're not serious about this guy."

Talk about coming straight to the point. Rick groaned. "You know what, Will? I appreciate you two seeing me home, but I really don't want to talk about this, all right?"

"Your timing needs work, babe," Blake said with a firm glance at Will. "Rick needs some space right now. Let him be." Rick gave him a grateful smile. His boss really did know him well.

"Just saying. That guy was acting so possessively, it was unreal." Will scowled.

"Will!" Blake snapped out his name. "Leave it." Will fell quiet and stared out of the window.

The rest of the journey took place in silence. Rick's head was in a whirl. He didn't know what to make of Julian's behaviour. It was nothing like the man who'd had dinner with him only three nights previously. He hated to admit it, but Will had pretty much nailed it. *Possessive* was the perfect word. *Controlling* might have been another, considering the whole menu thing.

Rick felt sick to his stomach. *I really wanted this to work.* Where it went from here, he didn't have a clue.

Rick sat back with a satisfied sigh. The 'Coming Soon' page of Trinity's website was up to date, as was the Bestsellers list. Their Facebook page had promos launched for all the new books that week, and his To Do list was full of crossings-out. Rick loved that end-of-the-week feeling when he could face a weekend, knowing he'd got everything done.

"That sounds like a man in dire need of a weekend," Ed quipped as he stuck his head around Rick's door. "You got anyfin' planned?" His eyes gleamed. "Maybe a fella or two lined up?" He leaned against the doorjamb, arms folded across his wide chest.

Rick smirked. "For a straight guy, you pay far too much attention to my sex life, do you know that?"

Ed guffawed. "Nah, mate. You've 'ad a busy week, aint'cha? I was finkin' you needed to let your 'air down, thas' all." He waggled his eyebrows. "An' never mind my crack about you linin' up guys. I 'ear on the grapevine you got yerself a fella."

Rick looked pointedly at Ed. "Do I come to your office and ask you about your latest bit of skirt? No? Then show me the same consideration." Not that he wanted to discuss Julian. There'd been nothing from him all week, not so much as a text. Rick was beginning to get that sinking feeling.

Ed snorted. "Point taken." Then a brief frown creased his brow. "'Cept that would have been a bleedin' short conversation. Don't seem to be 'avin' much luck wi' the ladies of late."

Rick batted his eyelashes. "Aww. My heart bleeds for you. Now clear off and let me finish so I can get on with my debauched plans for the weekend." He leered. Inside his head he laughed. Debauched plans indeed. Rick was going to spend the next two days vegging out in front of the TV with some takeaways and a whole lot of beer.

Ed snickered. "Then I'll leave ya to it." He gave a short salute and wandered off down the corridor, whistling. Rick shook his head, smiling. Ed was a real character. The coarse-mouthed, rugby-playing office manager came across as loud and brash, but Rick knew the truth. Ed would do anything for anybody. The man was like a big, cuddly teddy bear.

He shut down his computer and cleared off his desk, ready for Monday morning. His phone sat near the keyboard. Rick gave it a wistful glance.

Why don't you call him?

That was an easy one. *Because I wouldn't know where to begin.* The busy week had blurred his perceptions of their double date, but not enough so that he'd completely forgotten everything.

When the phone rang, it made him jump. But when he saw it was Julian, his heart gave a jolt.

"Hi." Rick waited, uncertain of what to say.

"Hey there." Julian sounded cheerful. "I just wanted to know if you felt like joining me at Heaven tonight."

Rick walked across to his window and stood looking over the London skyline. He leaned against the glass. "I wasn't sure if I'd hear from you again. And to be honest, after last Saturday, I'm not sure how

I feel about another date."

There was a pause before Julian continued. "This is about what I said to Blake and Will, isn't it?" There was an edge to his voice that hadn't been there before.

"Partly," Rick admitted.

More silence. When he spoke again, Julian's voice was softer. "Aw, baby, it was a joke."

Rick snorted. "Well, that wasn't how it came across." *To any of us.*

"You must know I'd never do anything to hurt you."

Actually, Rick didn't know that. "That's a good point. We chatted at Heaven, we talked during dinner, but we don't really know each other at all."

Julian's reply was immediate. "Then let's get to know one another. Please?" His tone was coaxing. "Look, we can meet up at Heaven tonight. Get our dancing shoes on, drink a little, talk some more. I bet you've worked really hard all week. You deserve one night to let your hair down and live a little." A moment's pause. "Please, Rick? Give me another chance?"

Rick couldn't help feeling flattered that Julian wasn't letting this go. *He must want this to work.* And besides that, Rick found it very difficult to say no, especially when someone was being persistent.

"Okay," he said at last. "What time?"

"Oh, great," Julian breathed. "Let's make it nine? That gives us both time to unwind a little after work."

"Fine." Rick tried to tell himself he was doing the right thing. "I'll see you there."

"Thanks, baby." He could hear the smile in

Julian's voice. "It'll be great, you'll see." They hung up and Rick put his phone into the pocket of his brown leather jacket.

God, I hope I'm doing the right thing. He did his best to put aside his concerns, and let his mind go back to that kiss they'd shared, his first impressions of Julian. *Maybe I'm making too much of Saturday night.*

God, he hoped so.

***

"Remember that bloke you were ogling two weeks ago?" Len asked Angelo as they waited at the bar. "You know, the one you couldn't take your eyes off all night?" He waggled his eyebrows.

Angelo hadn't forgotten. He'd looked for the gorgeous guy the previous weekend, but there'd been no sign. The fact that Julian Emerson hadn't been around either was a little worrying. Angelo didn't like the thought which nagged him. *Maybe they're off together somewhere.* It wasn't a pleasant thought. "What about him?"

"Well, isn't that him over on the dance floor?"

Angelo whipped his head around so fast, he got a crick in his neck. "Where?" He scanned the dancers, searching for that lithe body, those pretty blue eyes. *Bingo.* There he was, lost in the heady beat that pulsed through the floor. *Fuck, he looks even hotter than last time.* Angelo feasted his eyes on the guy's body. His tight-fitting red top clung to his lean form, and those jeans looked as though they'd been sprayed on. But what Angelo liked most was the expression on his face. His eyes were closed, arms moving sensually as he almost flowed to the rhythm. Angelo stared, transfixed by the peaceful look on his face.

"Why don't you go over there and talk to him? Buy him a drink?" Len suggested. He smiled. "C'mon, you know you want to." He dug Angelo playfully in the ribs.

Angelo laughed. "Quit trying to fix my love life." He was very fond of Len. His mate was a lot of fun and they always had a laugh when they went out to the clubs together. Angelo was there primarily to watch out for him. Len had gotten bashed a few years ago, and since then he was very wary of going out on his own. Angelo didn't mind accompanying him. He loved to dance, and Heaven was his favorite haunt. Len would go off and dance with his twinks, leaving Angelo alone to lose himself in the atmosphere. And if it meant Len could have a good time *and* feel safe? Angelo would do whatever it took to make his friend happy.

Len snorted. "You don't have a love life, remember? You're too fussy. You hate it when a guy comes onto you."

Angelo shrugged. "Can I help it if I like to be the one doing the pursuing?" His gaze was fixed on his Dream Guy.

Maybe Len's got the right idea. Maybe I should just wander over there and—

Fuck. Julian Emerson was with him.

"Aw, crap," he murmured.

Len frowned. "What's up?" He followed Angelo's gaze over to the dance floor. He scowled. "Oh God, him again." He shook his head. "I don't like that fucker. He gives me a bad taste in my mouth." Angelo quirked his eyebrows and Len flushed. "Not like that. I've seen the way he operates. A total control freak."

Angelo wasn't about to disagree. Julian had been a frequent flier at Heaven for about a year now. He watched dejectedly as the cute guy danced with Julian, although he had to note they weren't dancing all that closely.

I'm going to keep my eyes open, he thought.

Angelo Tarallo was a man on a mission.

Rick was having a good time. He had to admit Julian was right. This was exactly what he'd needed after the last week. And Julian was back to the attentive, personable guy he'd been that first night two weeks ago.

Maybe last week was a blip. Maybe this is the real Julian. He could live with that.

Julian gestured for a drink and Rick nodded. They walked off the dance floor toward the bar.

"You having a good time?" Julian asked him as he waited for a barman to get to them. Behind the bar several guys rushed back and forth, dodging each other as they served up countless orders, their usual banter reduced to brusque sentences as they focused on their tasks. Their smiled seemed fixed as they greeted the clients.

Rick smiled. "Actually, I'm having a great time." Julian beamed at him, and a rush of warmth filled Rick.

"Where did you disappear to, babe?" asked a familiar voice. "We woke up and you were gone." Oli stood next to Rick, Ben behind him. Oli's eyes danced with amusement.

All the warmth fled Rick's body. *Of all the times....*

Ben came up to kiss him softly on the lips. "There I was, waking up with a smile at the thought of a nice morning fuck, and you were gone." He grinned. "*And* we never got to thank you for the great night." That grin widened. "Or invite you for round two."

Rick was aware of Julian suddenly standing very still. *Oh fuck...*

"Sorry, guys," Rick said. "Can I introduce you to Julian, a—"

"His boyfriend," Julian interrupted, a thin smile stretched across his lips. The words sent a shock jolting through Rick. *My what?* He drew in several deep breaths, trying to control his emotions.

Ben and Oli shifted uncomfortably, which was probably nothing compared to what was going on in Rick's head at that moment. Oli lost his usual grin. "I think we've bothered these two long enough," he said quietly to Ben, tugging him away by the arm. Ben's gaze met Rick's. He could plainly read the sympathy behind those eyes. Ben gave him a smile and then a nod in Julian's direction. The couple walked off toward the dance floor.

Rick didn't know if he was shocked or furious. All he knew was that right now, he wanted some breathing space. He turned to face Julian, who stared at him, face unreadable.

"I'm going to the bathroom," Rick said simply and then walked away. He needed a little time to calm himself, and that wasn't going to happen with Julian standing there. A little cold water on his face, maybe a breath of fresh air, *then* he'd see how he felt.

The bathroom was empty. Rick turned on the

cold tap, cupped his hands under the flow and then splashed his face. The icy water stung, making him gasp. Face dripping, he reached for the paper towels next to the wash basin and patted himself dry. He leaned against the vanity unit and closed his eyes.

This is getting really fucked up.

Okay, Ben and Oli turning up like that was crappy timing, but Julian's declaration had him reeling. On what planet did one conversation at Heaven, one dinner date and then a double date make Julian his boyfriend? He expelled his breath in one long exhale, straightened and regarded his reflection. Julian stared back at him, leaning against the bathroom door.

Rick gave a start. "God, I didn't even hear you come in." Not surprising, he'd been so lost in his thoughts.

Julian said nothing for a moment, and then he walked slowly over to Rick and placed his hand on his shoulder. He leaned in close to whisper in his ear.

"You fucked those two, didn't you?" Julian dug his fingers into the muscle.

Rick inhaled sharply. "Whether I did or didn't is nothing to do with you. Have I asked you about guys *you've* fucked? Besides, this was before we met." Not that it was any of Julian's business. Rick shook his head. "And it's not as if we're going out together, is it?" Enough was enough. He met Julian's gaze in the mirror. "I think I'm going to go home. I—"

"You're going nowhere."

Rick gasped as Julian seized his upper arms and dragged him into a toilet stall, pushing the door closed behind him. Julian shoved him up against the partition wall, eyes blazing.

"What the fuck do you think you're doing?"

Rick yelled.

Julian grasped his jaw firmly, his fingers digging into the soft flesh of Rick's cheeks. He leaned in close, his breath wafting over Rick's face. "You're a fucking little tease, aren't you? One minute you're all wide-eyed and innocent, little Mister *'no I don't want to sleep with you on the first date'*, then I find out you've been fucking around that pair of sluts." His eyes gleamed dangerously. "Yeah, I know them. I know how they play." He dropped one hand to rub against Rick's crotch. "Well, *I* want to play now."

"Get off me." Rick tried to speak around that hand which gripped his jaw. His heart hammered wildly. Rick's head rocked back as Julian socked him across his cheek with a tightly clenched fist. Rick yelped in pain and surprise.

"Uh-uh," Julian said with a sardonic grin. "I think I've waited long enough to sample the merchandise, don't you?"

He pushed Rick roughly over the toilet. Rick put out his hands to prevent himself from hurtling into the wall. His heart was beating so fast he thought it would explode at any minute.

"Stop this!" he cried out, as Julian's hands yanked at his jeans. "I said *stop!*" The button flew off and landed on top of the closed lid. When Julian forced his jeans down and then ripped his briefs, Rick screamed, only to find Julian's weight pressed against him, a large hand covering his mouth. Rick was pinned, unable to move, unable to make a sound beyond screaming soundlessly into Julian's hand.

"Keep quiet and it will all be over before you know it," Julian said into his ear. "You never know, you might enjoy it." He kicked Rick's feet apart.

Rick shut his eyes tightly and waited for the nightmare to be over.

Chapter Five

Rick jumped as the door burst inward with an almighty bang. *Oh thank God.* A deep voice rumbled out.

"I heard him tell you to stop, so why don't you fucking listen?"

Rick was suddenly freed as Julian was pulled off him and he collapsed onto the floor of the stall, shivering. His body tingled as adrenaline flooded through him. Bile rose in his throat and he raised the lid of the toilet and heaved violently, hands grasping the cold porcelain. Behind him he was dimly aware of the sound of scuffling feet, loud cries and grunts of pain.

"I've got him." Another unknown voice. Julian growling. More scuffling. Rick wiped his mouth with the back of his hand, his stomach aching from the violence of his retching.

And then Rick felt a gentle hand on his shoulder. "Are you okay?" That deep voice again, only softer now. Another gentle hand, this time on his other shoulder, easing him away from the toilet bowl. Someone reached forward to flush, then closed the lid. Strong arms around him, lifting him, pulling up his jeans and tattered underwear. Those same arms turning him to seat him.

Rick came face to face with a man who bent low, still holding onto him. Black, curly hair, and eyes so dark, they were the colour of coal. Those eyes were filled with concern.

Rick breathed unevenly, his pulse still rapid. He lifted his head to meet those incredible eyes. "Th-thank you."

His saviour crouched low in front of him. "Just sit there for a minute, yeah? Get your breath back." He got to his feet, went to the washbasin and pulled out a couple of paper towels. After running them under the cold water and wringing them out, he brought them back to Rick and wiped his face with them. The coolness felt great. The man stroked Rick's unruly hair away from his face. "That feels better, doesn't it?"

Rick was about to thank his rescuer again when the door to the bathroom was flung open.

"Angelo, the bouncers have that creep in the office. They want to call the police." The voice sounded agitated. A second man came into view, roughly the same build as the man who was watching him so carefully. The second guy's eyes widened when he caught sight of Rick. "Hey, mate, are you okay? Don't worry, he's not gonna get away with this."

Rick's heartbeat sped up. "No...no police." He couldn't face that. His throat thickened at the thought of all those questions. His knees shook.

The man kneeling before him—*Angelo?*—stared at him with a dismayed expression. "You can't mean that. After what that bastard tried to do?"

Rick shook his head, teeth chattering. "But he didn't succeed, thanks to you." He swallowed heavily. "I...I'm sorry. Right now I just feel so ashamed." He lowered his head, face tingling.

Angelo reached out, his hand cupping Rick's cheek. Rick winced at the contact. Immediately Angelo pulled back. "You have nothing to be ashamed of, all right? I heard you. You told him no. Very clearly."

Rick raised his chin to look at Angelo. His stomach clenched. "Yeah. And he really paid attention to that." He drew in a deep breath. "Please, I mean it. No police."

Angelo sat back on his haunches, studying Rick. At last he spoke to the guy behind him, his eyes never leaving Rick. "Len," he said with a heavy sigh," go tell them this gentleman isn't going to press charges. They might as well let Julian go."

Len huffed. "I'll tell them. They won't like it, but I'll tell them." Then he grinned. "Although they may decide to be a little careless with their fists—and their feet—*before* they throw him out." He gave Rick a nod and then left the bathroom.

Angelo tilted his head to one side. "Want to try standing up?"

Rick nodded. "And the name is Rick, by the way. I'm guessing you're Angelo."

Angelo smiled for the first time since Rick had laid eyes on him. "That's right." He put out his hands protectively as Rick stood up, his legs trembling as he clutched his jeans around his waist. A wave of dizziness washed over him and he stumbled against the taller man, falling into his arms. "Easy there. I've got you." Those strong arms supported him. Rick was surrounded by a comforting aroma, the smell of fresh, clean cotton and spicy cologne. He drank it in, eyes closed, as he fought to regain his composure. He didn't even want to contemplate what might have happened if Angelo hadn't appeared when he did.

Angelo held him steady. Rick could feel his heart beating rapidly.

"Listen, I think it's a good idea if you go home," Angelo said after a moment.

Rick couldn't agree more. "Yeah, I'll call a cab." He still hadn't pulled away from the wide chest and shoulders which supported him. He couldn't explain his reaction to Angelo. Maybe it was the fact that he'd stepped in and rescued him, but Rick felt very safe in his arms.

Angelo shook his head. "I'll take you home."

Rick started to pull away. "No, it's okay, really." His legs nearly shot out from under him, but Angelo grabbed him just in time.

"I'm not going to take no for an answer," he said firmly. "But we'll have to drop off Len on the way. I can't leave him to get home on his own." Rick gave him a puzzled look and Angelo flashed him that warm smile again. "It's a long story." He fixed Rick with a hard stare. "So I'm taking you home. End of story." Then his expression softened. "Look, I promise, no funny business."

Rick sighed. If he were honest, he was relieved. His emotions were all over the place, and his body seemed determined not to cooperate. "Okay," he said softly. The beaming smile he got back from Angelo made him happy he'd agreed. Everything in him told him he could trust his dark-eyed rescuer, in spite of having trusted Julian just as quickly.

Besides, it's not like we're going on a date. He's just going to take me home.

After fastening his jeans, Rick leaned against Angelo as he led him from the bathroom, through the crowds that had gathered. Word had obviously got around. His cheeks burned as whispers and murmurs followed him.

Angelo spoke into his ear. "Don't let them bother you. If they want to rubberneck, that's up to them. Right now I'm concerned with getting you out of here and safely to your home."

Rick flushed with warmth. He put his head down and took strength from Angelo's arm around his shoulders. Angelo tightened his grip as they pushed their way through the onlookers.

I just want to go home. And then forget this ever happened.

Len was waiting for them by the office, and between them they ushered Rick out of the club. As they walked toward the car park where Angelo had parked, one thought sobered Rick very quickly.

Will is going to have a fit.

Once he'd left Len outside his building, Angelo pulled away from the curb and glanced at Rick. He smiled. Rick sat in the front seat, head slumped back against the head rest, eyes closed. A quick look at his chest rising and falling told Angelo the younger man was breathing more normally. Then he thought about it. He had no idea of Rick's age. For all he knew, they could be the same age. All the same, there was an innocence about that sweet face that made him appear young.

"Rick," he said quietly. No response. "Rick." This time a little more forcefully.

Rick opened his eyes. "Where're we?"

Angelo chuckled. "If I'm going to get you home, an address might be useful." Rick rattled off an address in Southwark, along with his post code, and Angelo programmed it into his sat nav. "Okay, go back to sleep. We'll get you home soon."

"'kay," Rick's eyes closed. Angelo shook his head. The poor guy had been through a traumatic experience. He wasn't surprised Rick was exhausted. Right now, sleep was probably the best thing for him.

He followed the instructions until he arrived outside a modern block of flats. He pulled into an empty spot in the parking bay to the rear of the building. Rick stirred beside him. Angelo got out of the car, walked around to the passenger door and opened it. Sleepy blue eyes gazed at him. Angelo eased him out of the car, locked it and then guided a stumbling Rick to his main door. Angelo watched him fumble in his leather jacket pocket for his keys, but he kept missing the keyhole.

Smiling, Angelo took the keys from him and opened the door. A staircase rose to the left of the entrance hall and an elevator stood next beside a wall of mailboxes. He steered Rick into it, who then leaned against the polished steel walls.

"Which floor?"

"Three," Rick mumbled. "Flat four."

Angelo pressed the buttons and the elevator whirred into life. The third floor turned out to have eight flats, but Angelo soon found number four. He opened the front door and Rick almost fell across the threshold into the lounge. Angelo could see the kitchen off to the left, and two more doors that were probably the bedroom and bathroom.

"M'feet feel like they've gone to sleep," Rick muttered. "Need coffee."

Angelo laughed. "Trust me, coffee is the *last* thing you need."

Rick pulled off his jacket, dropped it over the back of the couch and immediately flopped down onto it on his stomach, head nestled on a plump cushion, legs stretched out. His breathing grew more regular. Angelo stood and gazed at the beautiful man before grabbing the throw from the back of the couch and spreading it out over the now sleeping Rick. Angelo sat down in the armchair next to the couch, put his head back against the seat cushions and closed his eyes.

All his energy fled. He seemed to have been functioning purely on autopilot for the last hour.

If I hadn't followed Julian to the bathroom, tonight might have ended very differently.

The thought made him shudder. He still had no idea what had prompted him to follow Julian in the first place. He liked to think there was a mental connection between himself and Rick, that maybe he'd somehow sensed Rick's distress. He knew that was nonsense, of course, but it was all he had. His blood had run cold when he'd seen the empty bathroom and then heard the note of fear in Rick's voice from behind the closed door. That fear had Angelo frozen to the spot. Then he recalled the rush of cold rage that filled him when Rick screamed. *That fucking bastard.* He squeezed his eyes tight, but the scene from earlier was burned into his brain. Julian bending Rick over. Rick's jeans round his thighs, his briefs torn. A brief glimpse of Rick's bare arse as he lay flattened against the toilet by Julian's weight…

He'd grabbed Julian by the shoulders and yanked him out of the stall, flinging him across the bathroom. Julian had growled, and then stared up at him with eyes full of fear as Angelo had advanced on him, fists clenched. It had only been Len's timely intervention that had prevented Angelo from beating the slimeball to a pulp. Luckily Julian had been too dazed to put up much of a fight when Len had hauled him to his feet to drag him out of the bathroom, arms held securely behind his back. The bouncers had apparently met up with them outside and taken care of Julian.

Rick whimpered in his sleep. Angelo crossed the floor and knelt beside him, smoothing his hair and stroking his back through the chenille throw. "Shhh, easy, baby," he whispered. He sighed with relief when Rick's noises eased off. Angelo went back to the armchair and sat down, eyes fixed on Rick's inert form.

What is it about you? he mused as he watched Rick sleep. *Something* about him drew Angelo, that was for sure. He watched for several minutes before he realized it was getting late. *And if I sit here much longer, I'll be falling asleep too.* He smiled to himself. What would Rick think to wake up and find him fast asleep in his chair? After the night he'd had, Angelo could imagine Rick being more than a little freaked out. He got up quietly and with one last look at his Dream Guy, he let himself out of the flat as quietly as possible.

As he walked back to his car, Rick was still on his mind. Angelo came to a realization.

I don't want this to be the end.

He got into the car and sat there in the darkness, gripping the steering wheel.

So? Don't let it be. Do *something.*

He smiled.

Rick crept past the kitchen where Will and Blake were laughing and joking, and hurried to his office. He didn't want to talk to anyone, although he was pretty sure once Will caught sight of his face, Will would insist on talking. His right cheek was a mottled shade of purple. He'd stared at it in horror on Saturday morning when he'd gone to the bathroom. Then everything had flooded back. And again in the early hours of Sunday morning, when he'd awoken from a nightmare, dripping with sweat and shaking. It had been a long time before he'd been able to slip back into the welcoming arms of sleep.

He still couldn't believe that Julian had gone from being an attentive, sweet guy into the complete bastard who'd shoved him into that toilet.

Did I miss the signs? Were *there any?*

Sure, Julian had been possessive, maybe a little controlling, but nothing Rick had seen had indicated what lay beneath the surface. The Julian who had appeared in that bathroom was one Rick had no wish to encounter ever again. More than once over that weekend, however, Rick's thoughts went back to his rescuer. He could still remember how it felt to be surrounded by those strong, capable arms, the deep voice, the gentle manner.

One question rattled around in his head. *Where did you come from, Angelo?* Rick had no clue. He only knew he'd been damned happy to see him.

Rick booted up the computer and got out his To Do list for that week. He was going to deal with the turmoil in his head the only way he knew—by throwing himself into his work. He stared at the empty, clean mug on his desk. He was in dire need of a coffee, but that would mean braving the kitchen.

They're gonna see you anyway. Team meeting, remember?

With a sigh he realized there was no use putting off the inevitable. *Just get it over with.* He grabbed his mug and went toward the kitchen. The wonderful aroma of fresh coffee was like a siren call. He paused at the threshold and took a deep breath. As he entered the kitchen, he saw Blake kiss Will lightly on the cheek.

"Hey, you two," Rick called out, trying to sound as normal as possible. "No shenanigans at work, remember?"

The two men laughed, until Blake's gaze alighted on Rick's face. "What the hell happened?"

Rick walked across to the coffee machine and poured himself a mug, his hands trembling. As an afterthought he added two lumps of sugar instead of his usual one. He felt he was going to need it this morning. He turned to face his boss. Blake and Will both wore expressions of concern.

"I don't suppose you'd accept the '*I don't want to talk about it*' line?" he asked hopefully.

Blake sighed. "My office. Now. Both of you."

Rick matched his sigh and followed Blake out of the kitchen, Will at his side. Rick tried to ignore the rolling sensation in his belly. When they got to his office, Blake pointed to the comfy couch that sat below the window. "Park yourself there. Then spill it." He pulled up his office chair and sat, legs out straight, arms folded across his chest, still clutching his coffee.

Rick sat down, perched on the edge of the seat cushion, back straight, hands wrapped around his mug. Will sat beside him, his face unhappy.

Rick took a drink of his coffee, letting the liquid warm him. In a steady, calm voice he related the events of Friday night. When he got to the part about Julian in the toilet stall, Will bounced to his feet, fists clenched at his sides. His face was contorted in anger.

"I'll fucking kill him."

"Will, sit down and *calm* down." Blake spoke quietly. Will paused, cheeks flushed. Blake gave him a slow nod and Will sat down, breathing deeply. "Better." Blake turned to Rick. "Finish your story, 'cause I'm assuming there's more."

Rick swallowed. He related how Angelo had swooped in and saved the day, and then how he'd taken care of Rick.

Blake arched his eyebrows. "I like the sound of this Angelo. Was that the first time you'd met him?"

Rick nodded. "He was gone when I woke up Saturday morning. I have no way of contacting him to thank him properly." When he'd awoken early that morning, desperate for the loo, there was no sign of the good-looking guy who'd brought him home. He could still remember that warm smile. He'd touched the chenille throw which lay over him and smiled. Angelo was a thoughtful man.

"So what happens to Julian?" Will asked. Rick frowned and Will stared at him. "Well, tell me you're going to have him charged with assault, attempted rape, *something*."

Rick gulped. How could he explain?

"No, I'm not." Both men stared at him hotly. "Look, I couldn't face all the questions, right? Because if it ever came to trial, Julian's lawyer is just going to make out that I'm a slut who was asking for it. It won't matter that I said no. They'll just rake over my past, and bring up stuff that I'd rather have left alone, thanks all the same." He shuddered. "We all know how it works, yeah? I may be the one accusing Julian, but it's *me* who'd end up on trial. And I don't want that."

He stood up. "Sorry, guys, but I'm going to get back to work now. I don't want to talk about this anymore." As he passed Blake, his boss stopped him.

"You know I'm always here, if you need to talk. About *anything*."

Rick smiled at him. "Thanks, Blake. I really appreciate it. But right now, I think I'm just going to concentrate on my work and forget about men for a while. It's a lot less painful in the long run."

Blake gazed at him sadly. "It won't always be like this, you know."

Rick shrugged. "Maybe. I'm not convinced. Perhaps I'm just not meant to be happy, you ever thought of that?"

And with that he left the office, went back to his own, shut the door, and sat down at his desk. He stared at the computer monitor with its wallpaper of a gorgeous, barely dressed hunk, before right-clicking to remove it.

So much for wanting someone to love me, he thought. *Finding that someone wasn't worth this much heartache.*

Briefly his thoughts went to Angelo, his white knight. He shook his head and drained his coffee mug.

Knowing my luck, he already has someone. Maybe Len. And even if he was single, what would such a nice guy want with a slut like me?

This wasn't helping. Rick opened his folder and got to work.

Chapter Six

Rick only had to look at Lizzie wandering through the office with a huge smile on her face to know that things were working out with Dave. Considering their first conversation on the subject had taken place about seven weeks ago, he had to assume the couple had been on a few dates since then. He caught snippets of conversations as he walked past the kitchen. Rick was happy for her, he really was, but her situation only made him reflect on his own.

Why couldn't I find someone like that?

It had been four weeks since Heaven, and Rick hadn't been back. The way he looked at it, he'd tried to do the right thing and look where it had got him. So No More. He spent his weekends at home, watching TV or listening to music. When he'd gotten bored with that, he'd volunteered to help Blake out with his submissions. Blake was delegating a lot more these days, and everyone could see the difference. His boss seemed brighter, and was definitely laughing a lot more. Rick felt a lot of the changes were down to Will's influence. Will's departure from Trinity wasn't far off, and Rick was already sad at the prospect of not having him around.

Rick knew he'd changed over the last month. He was talking less at work, for one. He'd gotten into the habit of steering clear of the kitchen when it was busy, to avoid conversation. No one treated him any differently, but he could tell by the glances he was getting that his colleagues were concerned. Ed had taken to stopping by his office at the end of each day, to catch up with Rick on business. The blunt office manager didn't say as much, but Rick knew he was worried. In fact, it wasn't like him to be so reticent. Ed usually spoke his mind first and apologized later.

Rick was looking through the books due for release during the coming weeks, when the office phone rang. He glanced at the screen as he picked up the receiver.

"Hi, Karen, what can I do for you?"

"I've got a call for you. A Mr. Angelo Tarallo."

Rick became still. It couldn't be a coincidence. *How the hell did he find me?*

The receptionist cleared her throat. "Rick? Shall I put the call through? Or do you want me to tell him you're not available?"

Rick thought fast. "No, you can put him through." His heart pounded as he waited.

I don't have a clue what's coming.

"Rick? This is Angelo. We met at Heaven." There it was—that deep voice he remembered so clearly.

Rick smiled in spite of his racing heartbeat. "Like I could forget that." He heard a slight chuckle at the other end. "I have to ask, however did you find me?"

Angelo snorted. "It's taken me this long to track you down. I've been asking around at Heaven and every gay club I could find. All I had to go on was your name and your description, and where you lived. And although a few guys recognized who I was talking about, I still had to find someone who knew where you worked. I didn't want to turn up at your flat unannounced."

"You *have* been busy." It sounded as though Angelo had put in a lot of effort. "But why was it so important to find me?"

Angelo's voice softened. "I needed to know you were okay. I haven't seen you since then. In fact it seems as though no one's seen you for a while. It started to worry me."

All that, just to find out if he was all right. Rick was genuinely touched. "I'm fine, really. I haven't been to the clubs for a while because I've been…busy."

He could hear the note of relief in Angelo's voice. "Oh, thank goodness." There was a pause. "Look, you can shoot me down if you want to, but I wondered if you'd like to meet up."

Rick heard a noise and looked up to see Will standing by the door. He mouthed *Angelo?*

Rick sighed. *Karen strikes again.* He nodded.

"Rick? You still there?"

"Yeah, Angelo, sorry, I got distracted for a sec. Meet up with you?" There was the fluttery feeling in the pit of his stomach. Movement caught his eye. Will was shaking his head and waving his hands violently, mouthing *no, no.*

"Look, it's just for coffee, nothing more. I…I just wanted to see you again."

Rick's stomach did a somersault. It was on the tip of his tongue to refuse, but something stopped him. Part of him wanted to see the dark-haired Angelo again. There was just something about him. He drew in a deep breath. "Yes. That would be nice." He deliberately didn't look at Will, but he saw enough out of the corner. Will's wrinkled brow and restless stance said plenty.

When Angelo spoke, Rick could tell he was

smiling. "Oh, that's great. Is there a number I can reach you on?" Rick rattled off his mobile number. "Thanks. I'll send you a text to make sure I've got it right. I'll give you a call this evening. I'm sure you're very busy with work right now, so I won't disturb you any longer."

Rick liked the sound of Angelo. "That's fine." His phone warbled and he glanced at it. "Your text just came through, thank you." He smiled. "I'll look forward to your call tonight. I'm usually home by about six thirty."

"Until this evening, then." Angelo paused. "Bye, Rick."

"Bye." Rick disconnected and hung up the receiver. He rocked back on his chair, staring at the monitor.

"You aren't seriously going to go out on a date with this guy."

Rick looked up to find Will gazing at him with wide eyes. He felt his cheeks grow hot. "It's just coffee," he said.

Will shook his head, his mouth set in a firm line. "Rick, your track record with men isn't exactly awe-inspiring."

Rick's mouth went dry and the muscles in his abs tightened. "Thanks for reminding me."

Will sighed. "Sorry, but you know it's true." He folded his arms across his chest. "I think I should go with you."

Rick snorted. "Forget it. Not going to happen." Will pouted and Rick had to smile. "And that won't work either. Look, it's a cup of coffee, right?" He tried to ignore the butterflies. Rick wasn't about to tell Will that he hadn't been able to get Angelo out of his mind since that weekend. Will would only worry.

I mean, look what I thought of Julian.

Will was right. Rick didn't possess a filter when it came to the men he chose to hook up with.

And you know where that *got you,* he thought glumly. He stared at Will, unblinking, until Will left with a sigh and a shake of his head. Rick put aside any thoughts of Angelo and went back to work.

Let's just wait and see, okay?

Saturday afternoon at two-thirty, Rick entered the The Coffee Pot in Southwark, and he was half an hour early. It had been nice of Angelo to let him suggest someplace close to home, but by two o'clock Rick couldn't wait any longer. He'd wanted to arrive there early and maybe coax his stomach into calming down. But as he walked past the counter, looking for a table, he got a surprise. It seemed his coffee partner had had the same idea.

Angelo sat in the corner, looking damn good in a long, black greatcoat, fully opened and a white scarf which lay across his knees. Underneath he wore jeans, a soft-looking white sweater and black trainers.

Rick made an effort to breathe normally as he weaved his way through the tables and chairs to the comfy brown leather couch which was always his favorite spot when he came here. Angelo was perusing the menu and looked up with a start when Rick came to stand in front of the low coffee table. Angelo's face broke into a lovely smile.

"Hi there." His voice was rich, like cream. "I didn't expect to see you here so soon." He chuckled.

"Guess I'm not the only early bird."

Rick gave a nervous laugh. "I hate being late." He unfolded his red woollen scarf from around his neck, unbuttoned his brown leather jacket, and sank into the couch next to Angelo, laying the scarf beside him.

"I thought I'd wait to order 'til you got here," Angelo said, proffering him the menu. "What can I get you?"

Rick waved it aside. "I've been coming here so long, I know that menu backwards. I'd like a mocha, please, a large one." He needed the kick of chocolate. "And if they have any left, some of their homemade fruit cake. Highly recommended."

Angelo got to his feet. "Got it. Mocha and fruit cake." He grinned. "If the cake's that good, I may try some myself." He went off toward the counter and Rick settled back against the comfy cushion. The coffee shop wasn't that big, but it was very popular, especially around lunch time. He'd suggested three o'clock as most of the lunch crowd usually dispersed by then.

Rick couldn't believe how nervous he felt. It had taken him nearly an hour to decide what to wear, but eventually he'd decided on his black jeans and a rich red sweater. February had been bloody cold so far, and Rick couldn't wait for spring.

Angelo was back. He set a tray down on the table and then placed a big cup of fragrant mocha in front of Rick, followed by a latte for himself. Then came two plates. Rick recognized the fruit cake but the other contained a decadent piece of Black Forest gateau. Rick tut-tutted.

"A minute on the lips, a lifetime on the hips," he

intoned.

Angelo burst into laughter. "I've heard that one before." He pushed back into the corner of the couch with a contented sigh. "This is a nice place, by the way."

Rick echoed his sigh. "Yeah, it is." He picked up his coffee and sipped, inhaling the rich aroma. The cake could wait. "So, tell me about Angelo Tarallo," he said. He wanted to know more about his knight in shining armour.

Angelo drank some of his latte. "I'm thirty, and I'm an art restorer. I trained in wood carving originally, but nowadays I have my own business, mostly restoring wood carvings and statues in churches and listed buildings."

Rick stared. "Wow. That sounds very impressive. You must be talented to have your own business."

Angelo shrugged modestly. "I make a living. The statue work is more demanding, as I have to re-apply gold leaf and paint while making sure it's in keeping with the look of the period. I have my own studio, and I live in an apartment above that."

Rick studied the handsome face before him. "I have to ask, just looking at you... is there any Latin blood in your family? Because you don't look like someone whose roots are Anglo-Saxon." He chuckled.

Angelo gave a delighted smile. "Ah, you must be referring to my olive skin-tone and swarthy good looks." He winked. "My parents come from Sicily, along with most of my relatives. Many of them live in and around London. Mum and Dad run an Internet business, supplying Italian foods."

"Aren't Italian families usually very large?"

Angelo nodded. "I have three brothers and one sister."

Rick winced. "Oh, that poor girl, growing up with four brothers. Where do you fit in the line-up?"

"There's Vincente, Paolo, Luca and then me. They're all married and all with kids. Maria is younger. She's twenty-six." Angelo gave a fond smile. Rick guessed it was for Maria.

"With names like yours," Rick said with a smile, "do you all speak Italian?" The thought of someone murmuring to him in Italian during foreplay was very sexy.

Angelo sighed. "We all speak a little, I suppose. I used to speak it a lot, when I was little. Dad tends to lapse into Italian when he gets excited or angry about something. Watching him go off on one, ranting at full volume in frenetic Italian is something to behold." He smiled. "As I got older, I got out of the habit. I can't say that much, but when I hear it, I can pretty much understand quite a bit."

"What are your parents like?" He was fascinated. This was nothing like his family background.

"Mum is always smiling and having a laugh, except when Dad's in a mood." A crease appeared between Angelo's eyes. "Dad.... Dad is a typical Sicilian. He rules the roost. No one crosses him, not even Mum."

There was something Rick was dying to ask, although he had a feeling he already knew the answer. "Do they know you're gay?" he asked quietly.

Angelo snorted. "Fuck no." His eyes widened. "Sorry, I shouldn't have said that. The thing is, I know what would happen if I came out. I've already seen it. I have gay friends who come from Italian families. One guy's dad disowned him. Another lives here with his boyfriend. His parents keep asking him to let them come visit from Sicily, but he keeps putting them off." He stared into his latte. "My parents are always on at me to find a girl and settle down. It's partly why I've been staying away from family dinners these last few years. I get so tired of the constant inquiries about my love life. And that just puts me even more firmly in Dad's bad books."

He looked so forlorn that Rick couldn't resist putting out a hand to grasp Angelo's. He squeezed it tight before releasing it. Angelo looked down at it and then at Rick. His expression melted into that beautiful smile that Rick still recalled vividly from that horrible night.

Angelo leaned forward, picked up his fork and pulled away a morsel of gateau. His eyes closed as he savoured it. The tiniest moan escaped his lips. "Oh my God, that's heavenly." He pulled away another forkful and held it out to Rick. "Try that." His eyes sparkled.

Rick caught his breath at the intimate gesture. Unthinking, he wrapped his lips around the fork and slowly drew them back, his eyes on Angelo the whole time. Angelo's lips parted but no sound came out. "Delicious," Rick said, the words coming out more huskily than he'd intended.

Angelo gave a smile that was totally different in character to his previous efforts. This one was just plain sexy. He reached across with his fork and took a bit of fruit cake, and then fed it to Rick. "Is this better than the gateau?"

Rick swallowed. "I'd say...different." He gave himself a little mental shake. He was in real danger of getting turned on here, and that wasn't the plan.

Angelo seemed to pick up on his internal state. He reclined against the seat cushions and gestured toward Rick. "What about your family? Is it very different?"

Rick snickered. "Just a little." Then he reconsidered. "Well, we do have one thing in common. We both have a younger sister. Mine's called Maggie, and she's great. There's just me, her and my parents. I'm out, by the way, and they've been extremely supportive."

"You're very lucky," Angelo said wistfully. Then he straightened his face. "But tell me about Rick. All I know is your first name, and that you work for Trinity Publishing."

Rick cleared his throat. "My name is Rick Wentworth and I'm twenty-eight. I studied Media and Business for my degree, and I've lived alone ever since I finished college. I still go to family dinners, where my mother gives me the third degree over why I don't have a boyfriend." Angelo chuckled. "And if she had *her* way, she'd come with me on dates to check out all her prospective sons-in-law." When Angelo laughed, Rick shook his head. "Oh hell, I'm not kidding. This woman wants a wedding, grandkids, the works." They were both smiling by this point.

"It sounds like you have a wonderful family," Angelo acknowledged.

Rick dug into his fruit cake while Angelo polished off the remaining gateau. When he'd finished, Rick sat back and let out a contented little sigh. "This has been very pleasant."

Angelo smiled and his eyes lit up. "I'm glad," he said softly. "I didn't want to leave things the way they were." He gave Rick a speculative glance. "Except now that we've done this, I'd like more."

It was as if Angelo had read his mind. Rick held his breath. "What did you have in mind?"

Angelo inhaled shakily before speaking. "How would you like to go on a date with me? Maybe go see a film together, or a play? Or there's always the option of dinner." He watched Rick anxiously.

Rick studied the man beside him. So far, Angelo hadn't made a wrong move. If anything, he'd left Rick wanting to know more. It all boiled down to one thing: he liked Angelo. Liked him a lot.

I know I said I was giving up on men, but maybe I was a little quick off the mark. Maybe there is *hope after all,* he reasoned.

"That sounds lovely," he said at last.

The look of quiet joy on Angelo's face blew away any doubts. "Thank you." He reached for Rick's hand and clasped it. "There's something I have to say here." Rick became still. "I know we didn't meet in the best of circumstances, but I believe in thinking positively." His gaze met Rick's. "I'd like to get to know you, Rick. I think you're something special."

In spite of the initial shiver that ran through him at the reference to that horrible night, warmth radiated through Rick's body. "I'd like to get to know you, too."

Angelo beamed. "Would you like another coffee?"

Rick considered for a moment. *Stay here with Angelo or go back to my empty flat?*

"I'd love one."

Chapter Seven

"So, going to tell me how the coffee date went?"

Rick carried on pouring his first mug of coffee of the day. "Do you see me, Will? Am I standing in the kitchen in full view, instead of skulking in my office? I think you can assume it went okay." He turned around, mug in hand, and smiled. Will's words had been nonchalant enough, but Rick detected the edge of concern to his voice.

Will held up his hands. "Hey, I'm just looking out for you, okay? Because you were all smiles at the beginning with…" A pained expression crossed his face.

Rick sighed. He loved it that Will cared. "It's okay, you know. You *can* say his name. I won't break." He hoped his smile reassured Will. "And it was a good coffee date. I found out a lot about Angelo. And so far? He's a really sweet guy." Rick had had a good time. By the second coffee he'd relaxed. When Angelo had stood up to remove his coat and then settled back into the couch, Rick had to assume his date was relaxed too.

"Good. I'm glad," Will said emphatically. He fixed Rick with a firm stare. "Although I'm still going to check up on you, all right?" He grinned. "Have to keep you out of mischief, after all."

Rick picked up the tea towel and aimed it at Will. "Don't make me hurt you." He was grinning, however. Will pulled a scared face and scooted out of the kitchen. Rick chuckled to himself. He loved having

Will around, and it was a sobering thought that only scant weeks remained until he left. Rick was going to hold Will to his promise to stay in touch. He didn't want to lose his friend.

The Monday team meeting went like clockwork, as everyone reported to Blake on the state of their respective departments. Rick was back to his old self, laughing and joking. He guessed by the numbers of arm pats and warm looks he received that his colleagues had been worried. He could only guess how he must have come across this last month. That business with Julian had knocked the stuffing out of him.

At the end of the meeting, Blake asked him to stay behind. Ed was the last to leave, giving Rick a lingering glance as he left the conference room. Rick gave him a brief smile before Blake closed the door after him. Blake came back to the table and sat next to Rick.

"Don't panic, you're not in trouble," Blake said with a laid-back grin. "I just wanted a quiet word. How are you?"

Rick wasn't sure how to answer that. "What, in general?"

Blake scrubbed his hand across his cheek. "Actually, I meant in the aftermath of the Julian fiasco. Has he tried to contact you?"

Rick laughed raucously. "Like I'd answer the phone if he did." He'd done his best to drive Julian from his thoughts. The man had already taken up too much time and energy there.

"Good." Blake was nodding. "And how did Saturday go?"

Rick couldn't help smiling. "You need to

communicate with your PA once in a while, Blake. Will gave me the third degree this morning."

Blake looked relieved. "So everything is okay?"

Rick nodded. "Everything is fine," he said confidently. "Now can I get back to work?"

Blake gave him a playful cuff around the ear. "Get out of here, then."

Rick got up and went to the door. He turned back to watch his boss putting his various folders together. "Blake? Thank you." When Blake frowned, Rick gave him a gentle smile. "Thanks for looking out for me."

Blake waved his hand. Rick left the conference room and headed back to his office. Work time.

Rick looked around Pizza Hut with a shake of his head.

Oh hell. He doesn't like it. "Is there something wrong?" Angelo managed to get out.

Rick grinned. "I can't believe you suggested coming here to eat."

Shit. Their second date and already Angelo had cocked it up. "You don't like it here?"

Rick's grin widened. "Au contraire. I *love* Pizza Hut. But when you suggested going out for a pizza before the film, I was picturing an Italian restaurant, something authentic, *you* know." He glanced around at the packed restaurant. "I actually prefer this." He winked. "Does that make me a cheap date?"

Angelo sagged with relief. He laughed. "No, but it makes you an unpretentious date. I like that." He raised his glass of white wine. "Here's to Pizza Hut.

Long may they continue to serve stuffed-crust pizza and unlimited salad."

Rick clinked his glass of rosé against Angelo's. "I couldn't have put it better myself." He took a sip and then dug into the garlic bread and breaded mushrooms, making little enthusiastic noises.

Angelo watched him, smiling.

"So, have we narrowed down our choice of films to a reasonable figure?" he asked Angelo with a cute smile.

Angelo couldn't believe how similar their tastes were when it came to films. As a result, choosing a film was proving very difficult. "There was one film I didn't mention," he said slowly.

Rick quirked his eyebrows. "Oh? Do tell."

Angelo summoned up all his courage and blurted it out. "They're showing the restored version of Gone with the Wind." He held his breath as he awaited Rick's reaction.

To his surprise, Rick's face split into an enormous grin. "Really? I love that film!"

It was official. Angelo was in heaven. He expelled his tension in one long breath. "No kidding."

Rick nodded. "I love the book, and I have the film on DVD. I even have the documentary on the making of it, you know, the whole *who will play Scarlet O'Hara* bit." He dipped a mushroom into the sour cream and ate it with an appreciative moan. Angelo couldn't help smiling. This date was working out better than he'd hoped.

When their pizza arrived, Angelo asked for Parmesan, and then sprinkled it liberally over his slice. Rick watched him, eyes sparkling. "Got a thing for Parmesan, huh?"

Angelo chuckled. "It's something that was always on the table at home when we ate dinner. It was as common a sight as salt and pepper." He forked some salad onto the plate. The pizza was hot and delicious. He shook his head. "My mum has a fit every time she hears about me eating here. She says it's not proper Italian pizza."

"Does she make her own?"

Angelo groaned. "Oh God, my mother makes pizza to *die* for. Light, crisp base, juicy tomatoes, salami, mushrooms, mozzarella…"

"Stop it!" Rick wailed. "That sounds too good." Then he winked. "Although I do make a mean pizza myself."

"You cook?" Angelo lifted his eyebrows.

Rick huffed. "Hey! I'm a good cook. I love cooking, but I only like doing it when I'm preparing food for a bunch of people. Mum lets me loose in her kitchen sometimes when I go round for Sunday lunch. She loves it, says it gives her a rest."

Angelo took another mouthful of pizza and salad—delicious. "So what else do I need to know about Rick Wentworth?"

Rick stroked his chin. "Hmm, let's see. I like going to the gym about three times a week. I'm not a gym bunny, not at all, but I use the weights room." He flexed his arm. "Can you tell?" There was a teasing light in his eyes.

Angelo took in the nicely toned arms, the swell of his biceps visible under the dark blue silk shirt. Rick scrubbed up nice. "Yes," he said with a smile.

Rick's eyes widened at the word. His cheeks flushed. Angelo thought it an adorable reaction.

"Do you like your job?" he asked.

Rick sighed. "I *love* my job. I've been with Trinity for six years now. Blake is the best boss ever." His cheeks grew red.

Angelo was intrigued. "Tell me more about your boss, because I'd love to know what you were thinking just now."

Rick looked stunned. "Oh God, I blushed, didn't I?" Angelo chortled and Rick groaned. "I blush at the drop of a hat. And about Blake… It's nothing, really. It's just that I spent six years lusting after a guy I thought was straight. Then in walks Will Parkinson, and bam! Three months later Blake not only comes out, he goes and proposes to Will on New Year's Eve."

Angelo could only feel relief that Blake was spoken for. He felt a twinge of jealousy at the thought of Rick working with a bloke he plainly adored. "So your boss turned gay for Will?"

Rick shook his head. "Seems Blake has always been gay. He just stayed in the closet. Apparently Will was all it took to open the door." He smiled. "You should see those two together. Talk about loved up."

"And what about you?" Angelo asked. "Has there been anyone special in your life?"

Rick stared at his wine glass. "Me and long-lasting relationships don't seem to mix." His voice quietened. "The longest I've ever been with someone is about three months."

The expression on Rick's face tugged at Angelo's heart. It was an expression that plainly seemed to say that Rick wanted just such a relationship. Angelo forced himself not to jump the gun here. From what he'd seen so far, he definitely wanted to get to know Rick a lot better.

Take things slowly, he told himself. *There's plenty of time*.

"You didn't have to bring me home, you know," Rick said as they walked up to the main door of his building. It was already past midnight, as the film had finished late. *Well, it* was *nearly four hours long*. He unlocked the door and stepped inside.

Angelo followed him. "My mum brought me up correctly," he said with a smile. "And that means always walking my date to their front door." Then he snickered. "Except I'm pretty sure you're not exactly the type of date she had in mind." Rick chuckled.

The elevator arrived and they got in. Now that the date was over, Rick was on edge. Those rampaging butterflies were back, except this time Rick was sure they were all wearing Doc Martens. He had a serious case of déjà vu. The evening had been perfect. They'd talked all the way through dinner, and Rick felt as though he'd really gotten to know Angelo. The film had been great, especially when he'd leaned against Angelo, who'd taken hold of his hand and held it lightly. Angelo hadn't put a foot wrong. So everything now rested on what happened next.

Once out of the elevator, Rick walked along the quiet corridor to his door and stopped outside it. Angelo moved closer, until Rick could feel the warmth radiating from him. Angelo grasped the collar of his leather jacket and pulled him close.

"I had a wonderful time tonight," he said quietly.

"Me too." Rick hardly dared breathe.

"But I'd like to make it perfect," Angelo whispered and then he brought his lips to Rick's as he kissed him, so softy at first that Rick barely felt any pressure from that warm mouth. Then the kiss deepened as Rick melted into it, reaching up to place his hands on Angelo's wide shoulders. Angelo made a low sound as his tongue teased Rick's lips apart, slowly sliding inside to explore him. Angelo let go of Rick's collar and cupped his head and cheek, tilting him slightly to kiss him fully. Rick lost himself in the heady moment, submitting to Angelo's sensual assault.

When Angelo slowly broke the kiss and stepped back, Rick felt the loss instantly. His head spun, and he was acutely aware of his heartbeat, pounding so strongly. His fingers tingled with the need to touch Angelo, touch more of him.

"And this is where I say goodnight," Angelo said softly. His eyes shone in the glow from the wall light. "Thank you, Rick. I'd like to do this again."

"Yes." Rick's response was immediate. He wanted more. "Yes, please."

Angelo's beaming smile sent a rush of warmth flooding through him. "I'll ring you, okay? We'll sort something out for next week."

Rick could only nod, his throat tight. Despite his desire to stay strong, he wanted to take Angelo into the flat and keep him there till morning.

But Angelo's showing restraint, so I can, too. Because if that kiss was anything to go by, Angelo wanted him too.

Angelo kissed the tip of his nose and then turned to walk back to the elevator. Rick caught his arm and Angelo tilted his head. "What is it?"

Rick grabbed Angelo on either side of his head

and kissed him, moaning softly into Angelo's mouth as he responded, his arms coming around to stroke Rick's back through his jacket. When Rick broke the kiss, slightly breathless, Angelo grinned.

"You are far too tempting, Rick Wentworth. So I'm going to go now, before you get me to break my rules." He stepped back and pressed the button for the elevator, still smiling. As the door opened, he raised his hand. "Goodnight."

"Goodnight," Rick whispered as the door slid shut and the elevator took Angelo out of sight. He opened his front door and locked it behind him automatically. As he hung up his jacket, he smiled to himself.

This just gets better and better.

Then he thought about Angelo's last words. What rules?

Rick definitely wanted to know more.

"Okay, people, the last item for this morning's meeting is an important one, so I need you all paying attention."

Everyone around the conference table quietened and regarded Blake with interest. Rick wondered what was coming. Then he saw Will, who was almost bouncing on his chair. *Oh now what?*

"As you all probably know by now, Will leaves us in a couple of weeks." There were murmurs from around the table. Blake nodded. "I know, we'll be sorry to see him go, but I thought it would be good to see him off in a typical Trinity manner."

"Oh, *now* you're talkin'," Ed said with a grin.

"Party time!" Everyone laughed.

Blake held up a hand. "Yes, but with a twist. It's going to be a themed party, folks, so we wanted to give you plenty of notice to sort out your costumes."

"Costumes?" Rick echoed. "Oh God, I am *not* coming as a gay porn star, all right?"

Raucous laughter followed his words and he winked.

"Thankfully, that wasn't the theme Will chose," Blake said, his cheeks tinged with pink.

"Well, don't keep us in suspense," Peter called out. Beth nodded in agreement.

Blake grinned. "It's going to be a Doctor Who party." Will's grin was easily as wide. "So you can be as imaginative as you like. Will says he will loan out his precious Doctor Who DVDs if anyone needs some inspiration—which is pretty amazing of him, when you consider he won't let me touch them." Snickers and chuckles broke out. "And of course, there's always the Internet. So get thinking, people. I'm also inviting Dad and my friend Dave." Whistles broke out at this news. Beth and Peter dug Lizzie in the ribs, and her cheeks burned bright red. "I'll organize a bus to drop you off afterward, because I'm certain this party will involve a lot of alcohol."

Cheers greeted his words, followed by the excited buzz of chatter as the team started to share ideas.

Blake cleared his throat and silence fell. "However," he said sternly, gazing around the table, "it is Monday morning and we all have a lot of work to do. So let's save the planning for lunchtime, eh?" He smiled. "Have a good day, folks."

Everyone started to file out of the conference

room, still chatting animatedly.

"Rick, can you stay for a minute?"

Rick halted in his tracks. "Sure, Blake." He came back to the table. Will was still sitting there. Rick grinned at him. "Doctor Who, eh?" He shook his head. "That's sad, Will." There was no way he was about to reveal that his own DVD collection probably rivalled Will's. Rick was a Doctor Who *nut*.

"Oh, bugger off, you," Will said good-naturedly. He looked up as Blake closed the door. "Okay, tell us everything." He leered.

Blake laughed. "Well, maybe not everything, but we wanted to know how it went on Saturday."

Rick groaned. "I take it all back. You're not as bad as my mother—you're worse."

Will stuck up two fingers at him.

Blake was chuckling at the pair of them. "Enough, both of you. Rick, I take it everything went well."

Rick sighed. "You're not going to let this go, are you? Okay, I had a great time, although I was a bit wary at the end. I mean, I've been down this road before, remember?"

"I think it's good that you're wary," Will said. "Let's face it, you have every right to be."

"But it ended well, yes?" Blake pressed.

Rick nodded. "Angelo saw me to my door, kissed me goodnight and then left."

Blake made a noise of approval. "Oh, I like Angelo." He smiled.

Rick gazed at the two men thoughtfully. "Look, I need to say something here. I love the way you two are watching out for me, checking up on me, but honestly, I'm a big boy, guys. I can take care of myself."

"You know we're only doing it because we worry about you." Blake looked unhappy.

Rick gazed fondly at his boss. "I know. And I don't blame you after what happened. But can we just agree that if I need your help, or if I need to share something, I'll come to you?" He regarded Blake anxiously. "I've learned from my mistakes. I'll be more careful in the future, I promise, but I need to do this by myself."

Blake smiled. "Agreed. Along as it's understood that my door is always open to you."

Rick nodded. "Message received and understood."

He had the best boss. Ever.

Chapter Eight

Rick glanced at the clock. Lunch time. Humming happily to himself, he sauntered into the kitchen to grab his lunch from the fridge. As he poured himself a coffee and sat down to eat his heated pasta, his phone chimed. When he saw the screen, he smiled.

Dinner last night was great. Again, please.

Their third date had been dinner in an intimate little bistro, with soft music, candles, the works. And Rick had loved every minute of it. He sent a reply.

My thoughts exactly.

His phone chimed again.

Want to go see another play? Your choice this time, I promise.

Rick chuckled. Their second date had been to see a new musical in the West End. Musicals weren't really Rick's thing, but he didn't want to turn down the chance to spend another evening with Angelo. It turned out musicals weren't Angelo's thing either. And it had been dire. During the interval, they'd gone to the bar for a drink. When Angelo had said, 'Well, that was…different', Rick hadn't been able to keep a straight face. Angelo had taken one look at him and the pair of them had cracked up. When the bell rang for the second half, Angelo had grinned, grabbed his hand and they'd run down the stairs and out of the theatre, laughing.

Still chuckling, Rick replied.

Too right. I was scarred for life.

He grinned as he awaited Angelo's reply.

You have scars? I'll kiss them better.

The thought of Angelo kissing him sent tingles all through Rick's body. Because that man could *kiss*. Three dates, and three kisses on his doorstep, each one more intense than the one before. And yet Angelo still hadn't stepped over his threshold.

Maybe it's time he did, Rick thought. A frisson of excitement rippled down his spine. His fingers danced over his phone. His pulse raced as he clicked on 'Send'.

I'll keep you to that. Next date.

Angelo's reply was almost instantaneous.

Can't wait.

"You're not sexting your boyfriend, are you?"

With a start Rick shoved his phone in his pocket. Will stood by the coffee machine, arms folded across his chest. His eyes twinkled.

Rick picked up his fork and proceeded to eat his lunch, acutely aware of his burning cheeks. "You're too good at sneaking up on people," he said with a huff. "What are you, some kind of ninja?"

Will grinned. "Can I help it if you were so mesmerized by your latest message from Lover Boy that you didn't hear me come in?" He grabbed his and Blake's mugs and proceeded to pour out coffee. He sniffed appreciatively. "Your pasta smells really good. Which reminds me... has Angelo tasted your cooking yet? You know what they say, the way to a man's heart, 'n' all that."

Rick snorted. "Come on, we've only had three dates. And the farthest we've gotten is my front door mat."

Will stared. "You haven't invited him in yet?

Wow. You *are* taking things slowly."

Could my face get *any hotter?* Rick wasn't about to tell Will he was hoping that would change. Angelo had been the perfect gentleman, only now Rick was ready for more. "I meant it, Will. My days of leaping into bed with someone within hours of meeting them are over." He felt the flush spread up his chest. *Never mind that right now I really want to see what Angelo's like in bed.* He was curious to see what delights awaited him under the smart clothing. *Winter is such a pain,* he thought. *Too many layers. Give me summer when clothes are few and you can see what's under them.*

Will opened his mouth to speak but was interrupted by Rick's phone ringing. He fished it out of his pocket and smiled broadly when he saw the identity of the caller.

"Maggie! How you doing, sis?" He glanced apologetically at Will who waved a hand, picked up the two mugs and exited the kitchen. Rick cradled the phone between shoulder and ear as he washed up his plate. "How come you're calling me during the day? Is anything up?"

"Well, if Mohamed won't come to the mountain," she quipped.

"Excuse me?" Rick picked up his coffee, walked along the corridor into his office and shut the door behind him. He sat down at his desk.

"You haven't called me in weeks," she said. "I was beginning to think something was really wrong. I was just checking to see if your phone still works." He loved the sarcastic note in her voice. Maggie was twenty-three, still living with his parents and still a huge pain in the backside. When Rick told her—regularly—how much of a pain she was, she'd reply that's what little sisters were supposed to be, it was in their job description.

Rick flushed with guilt. He knew he'd avoided calling Maggie and his parents in the weeks following Julian's exit. They were the three people who could read him like a book: there was no way he could talk to them, let alone face them. They'd have known in a heartbeat that something was wrong.

And of course, you haven't called her recently because your mind has been on other things.

Well, *one* other thing—a tall, dark-haired, dark-eyed, Italian Stallion-type thing.

"Sorry, sis," he said sincerely. "I've had a lot going on, that's all."

She clucked sympathetically. "Well, Mum wants to know if you're coming to lunch on Sunday. And of course, she also wants to know if you're going to be bringing a guest." Maggie snorted. "She doesn't give up, does she? You think she'd have grown tired of your excuses by now."

Oh, now there was an idea…. Don't say it. Don't even think it, Rick Wentworth.

His heart raced. "Mags, what would you say," he began slowly, "if I said I was thinking of bringing someone?"

Maggie fell silent. Rick could hear the grandfather clock in the hallway, ticking away the day. Finally she seemed to find her voice. "Who is he?"

His heart thumped harder. "His name is Angelo. We've been seeing each other for a few weeks now."

More silence. "Bloody hell, Rick, you've never brought a guy to lunch before."

"And I might not yet. I still have to ask him if he wants to go." Rick's chest tightened. *Am I going too fast?*

He only knew that after coffee and three dates, he wanted to see where this would lead. And it was more than the allure of that gorgeous body. Angelo was proving to be a warm, thoughtful, considerate man. He tried hard not to get his hopes up, but the hope was there, all the same, and wouldn't be quashed.

"Ooh, wait 'til Mum hears," Maggie squealed. "This is going to make her year!"

Now he was worried. "Mags, please, tell her not to go overboard, all right? I don't want her to scare him off." He almost regretted agreeing.

"Oh wow." His sister's voice softened. "This one *is* important, isn't he?"

Rick swallowed. *Like you wouldn't believe.* "Yes," he said simply.

There was a moment's pause. "I'll tell her to go easy, okay? No bringing out the baby photos within five minutes of meeting him, that sort of thing, yeah?"

Rick laughed. "That sounds about right. So if you'll excuse me, I have a phone call to make."

Maggie chuckled. "After all this, he'd better say yes."

Rick prayed for the same thing.

"I'll see you both on Sunday. And Rick?" The love in her voice brought a lump to his throat. "I'm so happy for you. I'm keeping everything crossed that he's the one."

God, his sister knew him so well. And he had to tell someone. "I'll let you in on a little secret then, sis—me too." He hung up and then took a moment to breathe.

I don't believe I just did that.

Now all Angelo had to do was say yes.

He dialled the number and waited. After several

rings, a breathless Angelo answered. "Sorry, I'd left my phone upstairs in the flat. I was in my studio." His voice softened. "Hi there. This is a nice surprise. I don't get calls from you in the daytime."

His rich, deep voice sent a shiver down Rick's spine. "I wanted to make sure I caught you early on in the week before you got booked up," he explained. "Are you doing anything Sunday?"

"Why? What did you have in mind?" Rick loved the hint of amusement.

He crossed his fingers. "How would you feel about coming with me to my parents' house for Sunday lunch?" He closed his eyes and held his breath. He hadn't realized until that moment just how badly he wanted Angelo to agree.

"Seriously?" There was an undercurrent to his voice, something Rick couldn't read. His heart pounded. "Rick, I…I'd love to."

Rick had never felt so light. "That's great. I'll ring Mum and let her know we're both coming."

"How do I dress? Smart? Casual?" The note of anxiety in Angelo's voice was adorable.

"Wear what you'd wear if we were on a date," he said. Angelo was a stylish dresser. "That'll be fine."

"Okay." There was a pause. "Thanks, Rick. I'm looking forward to it."

"Me too, babe." The endearment slipped out without him thinking. *Oh hell.*

There was a pause. "I like that." Angelo's voice was soft.

There was the feeling of lightness again. "I'll talk to you soon, okay?"

"Great. Take care."

"You too." He disconnected the call, put the

phone down on his desk and rocked back on his chair. *Babe.* Rick liked that too.

Angelo stared at the red-bricked house, his heart hammering.

Please, don't let me screw this up.

In the passenger seat beside him, Rick reached over and took hold of his hand. "They don't bite, y'know."

Angelo huffed. "Well, they won't bite *you*— you're family. But me? That's another matter." He knew it was illogical to be this nervous, but ever since Rick had called, he'd been on pins. *This is a big deal.*

Rick chuckled. "Trust me, they're going to love you." He winked. "You wait and see."

Angelo bit his lip. *Oh this is just ridiculous. You're a grown man, for God's sake!*

Rick's fingers intertwined with his. It was an intimate gesture, but by no means an isolated one. It seemed to Angelo that each time they went on a date, the intimacy increased.

"If it helps," Rick said quietly, "I'm just as nervous as you are."

Angelo snorted. "I somehow doubt that."

Rick sighed. "You're the first boyfriend I've ever brought to Sunday lunch. Believe me, this is huge for me too."

Silence fell in the car. Angelo dragged his gaze from the house and stared at Rick. "Oh, *now* you tell me. Way to go, Rick. As if I wasn't apprehensive enough."

Rick let out a chuckle. He released Angelo's

hand and cupped his cheek. "Babe." Angelo quietened instantly. He loved it when Rick called him that. This was only the third time he'd done it, but each time it made his heart soar. Angelo stared into those blue eyes that captivated him constantly. Rick smiled and stroked Angelo's cheek. "Just be yourself and it will be fine," he insisted. "So how about we go inside so I can show off my boyfriend?"

Angelo took a deep breath and nodded, before reaching behind him on the back seat for the bouquet of fresh flowers and the bottle of red wine he'd brought. They got out of the car and Angelo locked it. Rick took the bottle from him with one hand and took hold of Angelo's with the other. He lifted it to his lips and kissed his fingers, before returning the bottle to him. Angelo had to smile. Rick used his key to open the front door. He led the way into the cream-colored hallway. Muted voices and laughter drifted from a distant room. Rick smiled reassuringly at him before pushing open a door and looking into the lounge. No one was around.

"They'll all be in the kitchen," Rick informed him. They passed through the hallway to the farthest door and Angelo took another calming breath before entering. Three people peered in his direction, a couple who looked to be in in their mid-fifties and a younger woman, who grinned when she saw them.

"Rick, I was about to call you and see if you'd forgotten the way. I mean, it must be all of three months since you were last here."

This had to be Maggie. Rick chortled and hugged her. "Behave, we have a guest."

Maggie smirked. "This *is* me behaving—badly." Her eyes sparkled as she approached Angelo, hand outstretched. "Angelo, it's a pleasure to meet you. I'm Maggie, Rick's sister."

Angelo shook her hand. "The pleasure is all mine, Maggie."

"Oh, a young man with manners," exclaimed Rick's mother with a smile. "And if my son had any, he'd have introduced you to his parents."

Rick pulled a face. "Mum!"

His mother laughed. She was shorter than Rick, with curly brown hair peppered with grey, and eyes that were so like her son's. She came forward.

Angelo held out the bouquet and bottle of wine.

"A small thank you for having me over for lunch."

Her eyes twinkled. "Oh, I like you, Angelo." She took the flowers and gazed at them appreciatively.

"I'll put those in water, Mum." Maggie took them off her and then went to the sink.

Rick's mother looked at the wine bottle and quirked her eyebrows. "A young man with taste, too." She handed it to her husband and then advanced on Angelo, arms outstretched, as she enfolded him into a warm hug. Angelo was a little taken aback by the exuberance of her welcome. When she released him, she looked him in the eye. "I'm Rachel Wentworth, and this is my husband Eric. We're delighted to meet you, Angelo."

Eric stepped up to greet Angelo with a firm handshake. "Pleased you could join us today." He and Maggie looked alike, both with black hair and blue eyes, except that Eric didn't have that much hair left.

"Lunch will be in about thirty minutes," Rachel informed them. She addressed Angelo. "I hope you like roast beef, Angelo. We tend to be rather traditional here when it comes to Sunday lunch."

"That sounds wonderful," he admitted. Just then his stomach decided to get in on the act with a loud rumble. He gave Rick a mortified look. Rick stared at him for a second or two and then burst out laughing.

"Don't worry about it," he said with a wave of his hand. "Wait 'til you hear my sister belching in her ever-so-ladylike manner."

"I do not!"

Angelo watched them do battle, albeit with affection. *When was the last time I went home for Sunday lunch?* He couldn't remember. He only knew he missed the verbal sparring with his brothers, his mother's cooking, the clamouring of his nephews and nieces…

Seeing this small but happy family welcome him with open arms was like a salve. Angelo pushed aside his nerves and pangs of guilt, and stepped right into the thick of it.

"I like him," his Mum confided quietly as she made the coffee.

Rick snorted. "I couldn't have guessed."

She gazed at him in surprise, cheeks pink. "What did I do?"

He chuckled. "You didn't stop talking to him all through lunch, for one thing. Poor guy was hardly able to eat."

She looked at him, aghast. "I wasn't *that* bad, was I?"

Rick hugged his mother tightly. "I'm joking. And it's nice that you like him. I happen to feel the same way."

She grinned. "To use your own words—I couldn't have guessed."

His Dad stepped into the kitchen with the plates and Rick stared at him. "You didn't leave Angelo alone with Mags, did you?"

His Dad smirked. "That boy can take care of himself. And personally, I think he's more than a match for Maggie's sharp wit." He gave Rick a nod. "I like him."

Rick sighed. "While you two set up the Angelo Tarallo Appreciation Society, my sister could be subjecting him to torture. I'd better go save that cute arse of his." He winked.

"Rick!"

Rick chuckled as he exited the kitchen. He loved shocking his mother.

He paused at the dining room door, where Angelo and Maggie still sat at the table, deep in conversation. From the looks on their faces, things had taken a more serious turn. He strained to hear.

"So you've only known him for a few weeks?" Maggie said, arms folded.

"We first met in January, but we didn't really get together until about three weeks ago, yes."

Rick waited anxiously to hear if Angelo would mention Julian, but his boyfriend left it at that. Then he thought about it. *Of course Angelo wouldn't do that. He's a born gentleman.*

"Look, Rick may seem the happy-go-lucky type, but a word to the wise." Maggie dropped her voice. "He's not had the greatest of luck with guys, so if you're only going to hang around for a short while and then dump him, you can sling your hook right now."

Rick caught his breath. He'd never heard Maggie

speak that way before.

Angelo smiled. "I have no intention of 'slinging my hook', he said quietly, "but I do intend on staying around. It would be nice if you and I could be friends." He locked eyes with her. "I appreciate that you're protecting him, but a, Rick is perfectly capable of standing up for himself and b, it would be unwise of you to piss off someone you've only just met. You know nothing about me."

"Is there anything about you that I need to know?" She lifted her chin, jaw set.

"Only that I care for Rick, very much. And that I would do anything to make sure he is safe and happy." His eyes glinted. "As you would do."

Maggie stared at him for a moment. Then her face creased into the lovely smile Rick knew so well. "You'll do, Angelo."

Angelo frowned. "Excuse me?"

Maggie shrugged. "It's obvious my parents like you. And the way my brother looks at you?" She snorted. "Yeah, that boy was never good at hiding stuff. So I had to make sure you could give as good as you got." Maggie smiled sweetly. "Think of it as a test. Which you just passed, by the way."

Angelo barked out a laugh. "Passed it? I'd say I aced it, wouldn't you?"

She squinted at him. "Don't get cocky." Then she grinned. "I like you, Angelo."

Angelo wiped his brow in mock relief. "I'd hate to see how you are with people you *don't* like." Then he smiled. "I like you too, Maggie."

Rick had to smile to himself. In less than three hours, Angelo had won over his family.

What's not to like? He's intelligent, personable, witty,

not to mention sexy.

Not that he expected them to concur with him on that last point.

And then something occurred to him. Much as he loved his family, he wanted Angelo to himself. And for once, he didn't intend on being left on the doorstep.

He was ready for more. Like, tonight.

Chapter Nine

"I love your family," Angelo said as they stepped into the elevator on their way up to Rick's flat.

Rick glowed. "Yeah, and I think it was pretty obvious they liked you. I thought Mum was going to start adoption proceedings at some point," he joked. He loved the way his family had taken to Angelo. By the time they were ready to leave at gone seven o'clock, it had felt so natural having him there, laughing and joking with Maggie, talking about his carving with Dad, and complementing Mum on her cooking. Right now, dinner was the last thing on his mind. He had other more pressing matters to think about.

They exited the elevator and walked along the corridor to Rick's door. When they reached it, Angelo pulled him into his arms and Rick responded without a second's hesitation. He was eager for the kiss he knew was coming. Angelo pressed him against the door with that firm body as he explored his mouth. Rick let escape the tiniest whimper, hands clutching at Angelo's back, pushing him harder against him.

Angelo broke the kiss, breathless. "I guess this is goodnight."

"It doesn't have to be," Rick blurted out. In the glow of the wall light, he saw Angelo's eyes widen. "Do you want to come inside for a while? It's only eight o'clock." He waited, stomach churning.

Angelo regarded him in silence for a moment, and then there was that beautiful smile that did strange things to Rick's insides. "I'd like that." His voice was barely a whisper.

Rick unlocked the door and led him inside, locking it behind them. "Would you like a drink? I have some white wine in the fridge."

"Better not. I had wine with lunch, and I still have to get home tonight. But I'll accept a coffee, if there's one going."

Rick smiled. "In this flat there is *always* coffee." He went into the kitchen and then called back. "Although it might be heated up coffee from this afternoon. That do?"

"That's fine."

Rick busied himself with the coffee in the microwave, trying to ignore the butterflies yet again. "I keep forgetting," he called out to Angelo, "you've already seen my flat."

He heard Angelo's chuckle. "To be honest, I didn't really pay much attention. I was too busy making sure you were okay and trying not to fall asleep in your armchair."

Rick entered the lounge with the two hot mugs, to find Angelo reclining comfortably on the couch. Rick smiled. "You look like you're right at home there."

Angelo regarded him with those dark, sexy eyes. "Come here." The words were uttered in a husky voice that went straight to Rick's cock. He put down the mugs on the low coffee table and then moved slowly over to Angelo and sat beside him. Angelo tut-tutted. "Too far away for what I have in mind." He grabbed hold of Rick and shifted them both, until Rick was lying on top of him, stretched out. Rick stared down at him, lips parted. Angelo smiled. "Much better," he whispered, before he cupped the back of Rick's head and took his mouth in a kiss that went from sweet to searing in a matter of seconds.

Rick groaned into the kiss, rolling his hips to grind against Angelo. He could feel the hardness of him. When Angelo pushed up, thrusting his tongue deeper inside him, Rick couldn't stop moving. He slid his arms under Angelo's shoulders and held on tightly as he began to rub against him, loving the low moans that spilled out from between those lips which devoured him.

They rocked against each other, the movement growing faster, more urgent, until Angelo broke away with a loud moan. He stared up at Rick with eyes so black Rick couldn't differentiate between pupil and iris. "God, Rick, baby, what you do to me." His voice was hoarse.

Rick groaned. "What *I* do to *you*? Fuck, I'm so hard right now, a cat couldn't scratch it." He grabbed Angelo's hand and drew it between their bodies to where his dick throbbed inside his tight jeans. He shifted, rubbing against him, and then moaned when Angelo gently squeezed his length. "Oh, yes." Angelo breathed heavily, fingers sliding along his denim-encased prick.

Rick couldn't take much more. He propped himself up on his elbows and locked eyes with Angelo. "Stay tonight?" His body screamed at him, hole clenching, aching to be filled.

Angelo became still. His hand movements ceased. He gazed at Rick, his mouth opening and closing.

Fuck. I moved too soon. Rick's heart sank. He started to pull away, but Angelo held onto him.

"Believe me, I want to say yes," Angelo assured him. "But I'm more than aware that you have work in the morning."

Rick's stomach churned. His body suddenly felt so very heavy.

Angelo cupped his chin and lifted it to look at him directly. "I'm not saying no, Rick. I'm saying...just not tonight."

There was a flutter in Rick's belly. Angelo's words sent a jolt through his body. "Really?"

"Really," Angelo echoed. "Maybe a Friday or Saturday night, when we'd have all the time we wanted to enjoy each other." He smiled. "I want to take my time with you. Savour you." He pulled Rick's head closer until his lips were against Rick's ear. "Fuck you all night long." The whisper tickled Rick's ear and sent all the blood in his body surging into his cock.

"I want that too." *Bloody hell, do I want that.* Angelo's words had him on fire. His body ached.

"Then maybe I should leave before you tempt me beyond my endurance," Angelo said with a wink.

Rick sat up with a sigh, trying to ignore his dick which throbbed with a life of its own. "Okay," he said, drawing out the word. He knew logically that Angelo's argument made sense. He was just having a hard time accepting it. After making do with his hand for over two months, the idea of a good, hard fuck scrambled his brain. But there *was* a part of him that wanted to delay the moment when they finally had sex. Okay, so it was a tiny part, and Rick would rather have succumbed to the overwhelming desire to get Angelo inside him. But he knew the anticipation would make their eventual union all the sweeter.

Angelo sat up and leaned forward to kiss him

softly on the lips. "Then let me drink my coffee and I'll be on my way. I might drop in on Facebook before I go to sleep, if you're on it." He grinned. "So your last thoughts of the day will be of me."

Rick laughed. "Oh, I can pretty much guarantee I'll be thinking of you tonight," he assured his boyfriend. He handed Angelo his mug and they sat there, drinking in silence while Rick let his body come back down from whichever plateau Angelo had sent it soaring. When he'd finished, Angelo got to his feet and held out a hand to Rick, pulling him up to enfold him in his arms. He kissed him, making it slow and thorough, until Rick melted.

Angelo backed away. "It's time to go, babe." He took Rick's hand and led him to the front door. One last kiss and then he stepped out into the hallway. "Sleep well, Rick."

Rick watched him until the elevator doors slid shut. He went back into the flat and closed and locked the door after him.

He didn't say no. Rick's heart sang.

He spent an hour or so watching TV, but he didn't take in a thing. His mind had a default switch that kept reminding him of the delicious sensations coursing through him as they'd made out on the couch. In the end, he turned off the lights and went to bed.

He sat back against the pillows, laptop balanced on his knees, as he loaded Facebook and clicked through his notifications. It was already ten o'clock but he wasn't tired. He glanced through his news feed, noting the posts from his favorite clubs which were advertising upcoming events.

The familiar chime signalled the arrival of a

private message. He grinned when he saw the sender. *Angelo.*

> *Angel: I should have stayed.*
>
> *Rick69: You okay?*
>
> *Angel: No. Pissed off. Horny as hell. Should have stayed with you tonight.*

Rick reached under the duvet to stroke his dick.

> *Rick69: You made me so hard tonight. But you were right to go.*

A moment passed before the next message appeared.

> *Angel: I wasn't entirely honest with you.*

Rick's heart skipped a beat.

> *Rick69: Go on.*
>
> *Angel: There's stuff you don't know about me.*

Rick's pulse raced.

> *Rick69: So tell me now.*

He waited anxiously, chest tight, as he tried to imagine what Angelo could have to tell him.

> *Angel: I've not had that many relationships, Rick. I'd start going out with someone, and then find out a little way down the line that they didn't want the same things I did.*
>
> *Rick69: Such as...?*
>
> *Angel: All they wanted was to fuck or get fucked. I wanted more.*

Rick couldn't believe it.

> *Rick69: Me too. Oh God, me too.*
>
> *Angel: Plus, they tended to be impatient when it came to getting into bed. They wanted to fuck on the first date. I don't do that. Sex is too important to be rushed into. I prefer to wait. Which pissed off a lot of them right there.*

Rick's throat thickened. Angelo could have been writing about him, prior to January.

> *Rick69: And tonight?*

Angel: Sigh. Tonight I wanted you. I've got to be honest here, Rick. I think we have something. But I'm in this for the long haul. I loved spending time with you and your family, but it just made me greedy for more. I want you in my life as a permanent feature, baby.

Rick found it difficult to breathe. Angelo wanted him. A slow smile crossed his face.

Angel: Rick? You still there?

Rick69: Still here, and newsflash - I want that too. *grins*

Angel: Yeah? YEAH? *happy dancing*

Rick was dancing right along with him. He hugged himself, unable to stop grinning. He couldn't remember the last time he'd been this elated.

Angel: Where are you? Right now?

Rick69: In bed with my laptop.

Angel: You naked?

That was all it took to have Rick's dick harden.

Rick69: Totally. How about you?

Angel: Yeah, me too. Was lying here, thinking about you tonight. How you felt on top of me. How hard your cock felt against mine.

Rick stroked his length slowly.

Angel: Wanted to fuck you so badly.

His hand moved faster, squeezing, tugging.

Rick69: Wanted you inside me, filling me.

Typing one-handed was so fucking *slow*.

Angel: If I had any sense, I'd come over there right now.

Rick's heartbeat sped up.

Rick69: What would you do?

Angel: Kiss you till your head swam. Stroke you, lick you. Lick your hole. Fuck you with my fingers until you were begging to have me inside you. Then fuck you through the mattress.

Rick's cock was rock hard again. Images filled his heated brain.

Rick69: Want you to do all that. Over and over again.

Angel: Typing one-handed is a bastard. You got a webcam? Got Skype?

Rick's world came to a dizzying stop. This was all new territory. '*Yes'* he typed, heart pounding.

Angel: Load it. Now.

Rick clicked on the Skype icon, his breath hitching. It seemed to take an eternity to load.

Angel: Can't believe I'm about to do this.

You and me both, Rick thought. Then the air was pushed from his lungs in a gasp as Angelo's screen appeared. It was filled with a nude torso, revealing a long, thick, very hard, cut dick. Only see the lower half of Angelo's chest to mid-thigh was visible, but his eyes were riveted on Angelo's hand as it moved slowly, stroking his cock.

"Am I turning you on, baby?" Angelo's voice wasn't as full as usual, coming through the speakers of the laptop, but the husky quality sent shivers running through him. "Forget I asked. I can see by your face that I am."

"Fuck, yes." Rick was mesmerized. Angelo's dick was beautiful.

Angelo chuckled. "You're not playing fair. The name of this game is 'I show you mine, you show me yours.' So show me. Let me see you."

Rick pushed back the duvet and placed the laptop to one side, arranging it until all that showed in the tiny screen in the corner was his cock pointing skyward, his hand wrapped around it.

"Fuck, Rick, you have a lovely dick. Wish I was there right now to taste it."

Oh, *that* set his hips rolling, pushing up off the bed.

"You ever done this before?" Angelo asked, his hand tugging gently at his cock, moving from root to head, adding a little twist at the end.

"No." Rick was equally breathless. "Had phone sex a few times, and got someone off via Facebook Chat, but webcams? Never."

That hand moved faster, as a second came into view, stroking his balls. "Want to fuck you right now." There was a pause. "Move the laptop, Rick. Let me see your hole. Want to watch you slide a finger inside you." The urgency in his voice was compelling.

Rick obeyed without hesitation. He threw back the duvet and placed the laptop on the mattress, adjusting the angle of the cover until his screen showed his groin up close and personal. As an afterthought, he stuffed a pillow under his arse so that his hole was clearly visible.

"How's that?" he asked, voice rough with desire.

"Oh fuck." Angelo spoke softly. "God, I want to be there with you. You're gorgeous, baby."

Rick glowed. He reached into the drawer next to his bed and took out the lube. He slicked up a couple of fingers and then slid them down over his balls to where his hole pulsed. He cupped his sac and let the digit slide into that tight channel. Rick groaned.

"Tell me how it feels," Angelo demanded. "Talk to me."

"Feels hot and tight." Rick gazed at the screen where Angelo was tugging his balls. "I'm imagining it's your finger, sliding into me." He added another, moaning as his fingers grazed his prostate.

"Feels so good, doesn't it?" Rick could hear the

excitement in Angelo's voice. "You got any toys? A dildo, maybe?"

That sent the muscles tightening around his fingers. "I've got a great dildo. Long and thick, just like your dick."

"Perfect." Angelo was almost purring. "Get it, babe. Get it slick."

Rick pulled free of his body and reached once more into the drawer. His hand found the sturdy cock and pulled it out hurriedly. He dribbled lube over the length of it.

"Hurry, baby," Angelo's voice urged. "I'm so close. I want us to come together."

Rick knew it would only take a few strokes of the dildo inside him and he'd be coming too. He placed the wide head of the realistic-looking cock against his hole and slowly, *slowly* pushed it into that hot tightness. He moaned long and low as it filled his channel. It had a nice girth, maybe six inches, and long enough to make sure he knew about it.

"Oh bloody hell." Angelo groaned. Rick could see pre-come leaking already from Angelo's dick, a long, delicate strand that caught the light as it spun out from his slit. "Now fuck yourself with it, as deep as you can take it. That's my cock inside you, Rick. Feel me fucking you? Sliding into you?"

Rick panted as he fucked himself with the dildo, hips bucking, his hand moving faster on his shaft.

"Fuck, you're beautiful like this. Can't wait till I'm deep inside you, kissing you while I shove my hard-as-fuck dick as far in you as it's possible to go."

Rick felt the familiar tingle in his balls. "Going to come." He watched Angelo move faster, until his hand was almost a blur. He pulled at his cock, desperate for release.

"That's it, baby, come for me. Want to see you come. Want to hear my name on your lips as you orgasm. Shout it, Rick, let me hear you." Angelo panted fiercely now. "Oh fuck, I'm coming. God, Rick!" Rick watched as come pulsed from his dick, spattering his chest and abs. Angelo trembled, breathless as his orgasm overtook him.

His name on Angelo's lips as he came sent Rick tumbling over the edge. His arse clenched around the dildo as he spurted into the air, showering his body with warm drops of the creamy fluid. He cried out, unable to hold it back. "Angelo!" His body was jolted as his orgasm rocked through him, back arched up off the bed, thighs shaking. He dropped back onto the mattress and reached for the laptop, dragging it until his face filled his screen. He looked shattered, perspiration on his brow—and that well-fucked look that he hadn't seen for ages.

Angelo obviously had the same idea. His face came into view. Angelo grinned back at him.

"That was the hottest thing I have ever seen," he said hoarsely. "I only wish I could have seen your face as you came. Because hearing you shout my name was incredible."

Rick strove to breathe normally. He turned onto his side and stared at Angelo. "Next time, yeah? I want the real thing. No webcams, just the two of us. And maybe it'll be my turn to fuck you." His softened cock started to fill at the thought. Rick chuckled. "Because if this is what we're like on webcam, can you imagine what it will be like in the flesh?"

Angelo's smile was huge. "That's easy. It will be even better."

Rick couldn't wait.

Chapter Ten

Friday night. Work had finished at five thirty and everyone had disappeared to get into their costumes. Rick couldn't wait to see them. He'd chosen the dark blue suit and long coat of the tenth Doctor Who, David Tennant. He'd even printed out a picture of the Doctor's sonic screwdriver, cut it out and stuck it onto cardboard. Ed and Blake had set up all the food and drink, and judging by the amount of alcohol Rick had seen, he figured Blake had invited more guests. Because if all that was just for Blake and his team, plus Dave and Justin? Rick would be going home *very* drunk.

He'd already spoken with Angelo that day. Rick had been in two minds whether to invite him along, but when Angelo had asked if other partners were attending, Rick had been forced to admit that wasn't the case. Angelo had chuckled, and told him there'd be plenty of other occasions in the future. Rick had to smile at that. Angelo was the perfect counterbalance to his impetuosity.

Rick walked into the conference room. "Ta-daaa!"

Will beamed. "All right! My favorite Doctor!" Then he scowled. "Now I'm jealous. I wanted to come as David Tennant, but could I find a costume anywhere?" He'd come as Matt Smith, complete with red fez and bow tie.

Rick flushed guiltily. "Oops. Sorry."

Will smiled good-naturedly. "It's okay, at least

someone came as him. Want to give me a hand setting up the screen?" He'd brought along his DVDs and was going to show them, without sound, throughout the party. The Doctor Who theme music was on a loop, playing in the background.

Justin Davis arrived at six-thirty, looking resplendent in a long, red overcoat, floppy wide-brimmed hat and ridiculously long knitted scarf. Will burst into applause when he caught sight of his future father-in-law.

"Tom Baker, as I live and breathe!"

Justin gave a short bow.

Will smiled broadly at Justin. "Thank you so much. You look brilliant."

Justin hugged Will briefly. "Well, we had to make an effort for your send-off, right?" He looked around. "And where is that son of mine? What's his costume like?"

Will snorted. "I wish I knew. He's kept it a secret."

The door opened and Blake entered, dressed completely in black, complete with black cape and a stuck-on goatee beard. He did a twirl, his cape swirling around him dramatically.

Rick was delighted. "Oh my God, it's the Master!" Justin looked puzzled, so Rick hastened to tell him the Master had been an early adversary of the Doctor's.

"What do you think?" Blake asked his fiancé, stroking his false beard.

Will's face glowed. "I think you look wonderful." His voice was soft. He cupped Blake's cheek and kissed him, his lips lingering there.

Justin cleared his throat and both men broke

apart, cheeks flushed.

Rick smiled with glee. It was going to be a great party.

It was nearly midnight and the party was drawing to a close. The bus was due in about twenty minutes and the food had been consumed, along with most of the alcohol. Will had plainly had a wonderful night. He'd danced with everyone, including Justin, which had raised a lot of laughs. Justin seemed so much more relaxed now he'd officially stepped away from the business. And it was clear he thought very highly of his soon-to-be son-in-law.

Rick had had a great night. Ed's costume had stolen the show. He'd appeared in a motorized wheelchair which he'd dressed up to look like Davros's console, and then Ed had sat in it, dressed in a shiny black suit, his face hidden by a revolting mask. The mask had lasted all of thirty minutes, after which period of time Ed had realized he couldn't drink fast enough through a straw, and off it had come.

"We're gonna stay in touch, right?" Will said indistinctly, his arm around Rick's shoulder. He was definitely the worse for wear.

Rick gave a drunken chuckle. "Yeah, 'course we are, mate. Besides, I love ya. Not lettin' ya get away that easily."

Will sighed into his ear. "Never did tell, you know?"

Even in his inebriated state, Rick knew what *that* meant. Will was the only one at work who knew Rick had had the hots for Blake. He kissed Will on the cheek. "Thanks, mate. 'preciated."

"Any time." Will wrapped his arms around Rick and hugged him. "An' if you ever need me, I'll be there for you, okay?"

Rick smiled. He was going to miss his friend, but he had a feeling Will wouldn't be going far. And for that he was glad.

"So how was the party last night? Was it good?" Angelo asked, raising his voice to be heard above the pulsating rhythms of G-A-Y. He grinned. "Or should I be asking, how is your head tonight?" Rick certainly looked slightly rougher around the edges.

Rick groaned. "I've had a headache for most of today, *that's* how good the party was."

Angelo made a sympathetic noise. "Poor baby." Then he grinned again. "I have no sympathy for self-induced misery. But I'm glad you had a good time." He kissed Rick on top of his head.

Rick smiled, grabbed hold of his hand and led him to one of the booths where it was quieter. He pulled Angelo next to him and then leaned in to kiss him, slowly at first, but then with increasing intensity as both men got into it. Angelo mined his mouth with a probing tongue, tasting him deeply. In his head all he could see was Rick, wantonly fucking himself with that dildo, come spurting like a fountain. He groaned and pushed deeper. Rick moaned, the sound reverberating through him, until suddenly he was pushing at Angelo's chest with both hands.

Angelo released his mouth and sat back, breathless. "Am I doing something wrong?"

Rick snorted. "Oh God, no, you're doing something *right*. It's just that if I let this go on, we'd get arrested for performing a lewd or indecent act in public."

Angelo leaned forward and nuzzled the warm, soft skin of Rick's neck, where the scent of his boyfriend was at its most potent. That warm, earthy smell did delicious things to his body. And after what they'd engaged in last Sunday night, Angelo wasn't afraid to give voice to his needs. "Want you," he ground out, hand slipping down to caress Rick's crotch. Rick jerked, pushing his erection into Angelo's palm. Oh yeah, Rick wanted him too.

"Have I told you how much I enjoyed what we did last Sunday?" Rick said, panting.

Angelo chuckled against his neck. "You might have, once or twice." It had made for some very interesting phone conversations that week.

Rick groaned. "Do you know how difficult it is to focus when you do that?"

"So focus on this instead," Angelo whispered as he stroked Rick's heavy shaft a little faster.

"Christ, enough!" Rick broke away, gasping. "What I was *trying* to say—until you started distracting me with those sneaky fingers—is that I want you to come home with me tonight." His cheeks burned. "And stay the night."

Angelo stared at him. "You sure?"

Rick rolled his eyes. "Sure? Did you just have your hand on my dick? Could I have *been* any harder?" Angelo smirked. "What I'm trying to tell you is, lovely as Sunday was, I want the real thing tonight. You, in my bed, in me."

Angelo caught his breath at the image conjured

up by those few words.

Rick was grinning smugly. "Is that a yes?"

Angelo pushed Rick back against the padded seat and plundered that hot mouth, his tongue virtually down Rick's throat. Rick brought up his arms to grab hold of Angelo's shoulders, squirming beneath him, hips rolling as he moaned hungrily. Angelo broke the brutal kiss and sat back with a grin. "Does that answer your question?"

Rick's eyes gleamed with lust. "What are we sitting here for, then? Let's get out of here." He was on his feet in seconds, almost bouncing with excitement as he tugged Angelo to join him. Angelo laughed, trying not to trip over his own feet as Rick pulled him through the crowds, past the bar and out onto the street.

"That was the fastest I've ever gotten out of there," Angelo admitted with a snicker. "Keep your eyes peeled for a taxi." He'd left the car at home tonight.

"We'll have better luck at the other end of the street," Rick told him. "There are more clubs up that way and more chance of finding a taxi." He held out his hand toward Angelo.

Angelo stared at it for a moment and then intertwined his fingers with Rick's. They walked along the pavement, hand in hand. The noise from the gay bar receded into the background. It was one in the morning, and most of the clubs weren't ready to disgorge their patrons out onto the streets just yet. The air was fresh, with a little bite to it as the breeze blew along the street, whipping up litter and making it dance along the gutters.

"This is nice," he said quietly. Rick turned to

him, head tilted, eyes questioning. Angelo raised their interlaced hands. "This," he said simply.

Rick's expression morphed into a look of contentment. "Yeah, it is," he agreed, smiling. Angelo tightened his fingers around Rick's, the happiest he'd felt in a long time.

They got to the end of the street where the noise level increased. Angelo spotted an empty taxi waiting across the road and was about to point this out to Rick when he saw something that made the blood freeze in his veins. Coming across the road toward him, surrounded by a group of raucous, braying men, was his brother Luca. And Luca was staring down at their joined hands.

Oh fucking hell, no.

Luca's face was a mask of shock. And then it changed. His lip curled, his eyes grew flinty and cold and his nostrils flared.

Angelo had to get them out of there, *now*. He tightened his grip on Rick's hand and sprinted across the street.

"Hey, what's the rush?" Rick exclaimed, laughing. "You *that* eager to get me into bed?" His voice carried on the air, and Angelo had just enough time to see Luca's head jerk, before he yanked open the taxi door and all but pushed Rick inside. He barked out Rick's address and then sat back, trying to melt into the dark interior of the cab as it pulled away from the curb. As they drove past, his brother followed its progress with his eyes, talking animatedly with his mates, whose heads swivelled to look after them. Angelo twisted around to stare through the rear window, in time to see Luca shouting something at him soundlessly, face contorted in disgust.

Angelo sank into the seat, his heart pounding so fast, he swore he was about to have a heart attack. Beside him, Rick hummed happily to himself, blissfully unaware of the turmoil in Angelo's head. All thoughts of what they'd planned fled, leaving him cold inside. Only one thought was burning into his agitated brain.

Luca will tell Mum and Dad. There's no way he's going to keep something this huge to himself. He thought back over exactly what Luca had seen—him walking, hand in hand with another man. There weren't too many ways that could be interpreted. Angelo pictured Luca as he'd passed him, recalling the movement of his lips as he'd yelled at him. With a shock, he realized he knew what Luca had been saying. It was a word in Italian. *Finocchio.* Fag.

For the rest of the journey to Southwark, Angelo sat in silence. *What the fuck do I do now?* Maybe he could talk to Luca, before he had a chance to get to his parents. They'd been close when the boys had been younger, but when Luca had married and then they'd had a baby, he'd found he had less and less in common with his older brother.

What the hell was a married man doing coming out of clubs at one in the morning anyway? Not that it mattered. Luca was married, with a child, both things putting him firmly in Dad's good books. Unlike Angelo.

"Hey, what planet are *you* on, babe?"

Angelo gave a start. The taxi had come to a stop outside Rick's building. Rick grinned at him and opened the door to get out. Angelo caught his arm, stopping him. Rick turned to him in surprise.

"Listen, I'm not feeling so good," Angelo said quietly.

Rick's eyes grew round. The expression of

concern he saw there made Angelo feel like a complete and utter bastard. "Oh, I'm sorry. Do you want to call it off and go home?" Angelo could see Rick was torn, but there was no way he could be around his boyfriend right now. He was never that good at masking his emotions, and the thought of trying to hide what was going on his head made his stomach clench until it felt as hard as stone.

"Yeah, I think that's best." He leaned forward and kissed Rick on the lips. "Go on in, go to bed and get some sleep. I'll call you tomorrow, okay?"

Rick nodded. "I'll miss you tonight," he said softly. He attempted a half-hearted smile.

Angelo's smile matched his. "Me too." He kissed him once more and then sat back in the seat. Rick got out of the taxi and stood, waving as it pulled away. Angelo turned around to wave at him through the rear window. There was no mistaking the look of sadness on Rick's face, although it was clear he was trying to hide it.

Oh baby. I'm getting a very bad feeling about this.

Angelo had that sinking feeling it was only going to get worse

When dawn came, Angelo was staring up at his bedroom ceiling, wide awake and exhausted. Each time he'd gotten close to dropping off, he'd seen Luca, face contorted, the cords in his neck standing out, fists clenched. And shouting that hateful word. It was a word Angelo had heard a lot as he was growing up. It passed his father's lips often enough to be burned indelibly into his memory. *Finocchio.* Yeah, all Dad's kids knew the meaning of *that* one.

By the time eight o'clock arrived, he knew it was pointless lying in bed. He got up and padded naked into his bathroom, mechanically going through the motions. Then he walked into the kitchen and set up his coffee machine. As he stood waiting for the coffee to brew, he couldn't stop the relentless, restless tumbling of his thoughts.

Maybe I should go down to the studio and carve some wood, channel my energy into something positive and creative. The idea brought a small measure of calm—until his phone rang, shattering the quiet of his flat. When he looked at the screen, a wave of nausea rolled over him. *Dad.*

For one split second he thought of ignoring it. Until he realized this wasn't going to go away. He picked up his phone and connected the call.

"Morning, Dad. Is everything okay? You don't usually call me this early." The words sounded hollow. His father never called him. That task was left to his mother.

"You will be at the house within the hour. Is that understood?"

That was his father, never one to waste time.

"Dad, I'm sorry but today isn't very convenient," he lied. "I'm going to be working on a project in my stu—"

"Here. Within the hour." His father hung up.

Angelo stared at the phone in horror. His stomach heaved and he ran to the bathroom, sinking to his knees in front of the toilet just in time as he retched into the bowl, stomach aching and sore. When he was sure there was nothing left to come out, he sat back on his haunches, tore off some toilet paper and wiped his mouth.

Shakily he got to his feet and went to the basin to wash his hands and face in cool water. He stared at his face in the mirror, noting the tiny red spots below his eyes, burst blood vessels due to the violence of his vomiting.

This was not going to end well.

Chapter Eleven

Angelo switched off the engine and sat, hands resting on the steering wheel. He'd had to rush as fast as he could through London to Primrose Hill where his parents resided in a large, sprawling house. He'd made it within the hour, but right now, he needed to summon up all his courage just to walk through the front door.

No use putting off the inevitable, he told himself.

He got out of the car, locked it and walked slowly up to the large, ornate front door. As he raised his hand to ring the bell, the door opened and his brother Vincente stood there, face unreadable. Angelo stared in surprise to find him there. He opened his mouth to speak but Vincente beat him to it.

"Dad's waiting for you in the dining room."

Angelo waited for his eldest brother to say something more, but Vincente stared at him in silence, standing to one side to let him pass. Angelo stepped into the wide hallway, his heart sinking more and more with each step. He paused at the threshold to the dining room before pushing open the door—and then froze when he saw what awaited him.

Gathered around the huge, rectangular oak table were all his brothers, his sister and at the head of the table, his parents.

Oh my God, a fucking family meeting. Except it looked—and felt—more like the Inquisition.

"Sit down." His father pointed to the empty chair at the other end of the table.

There was nothing to do but obey. Angelo took his seat as Vincente slipped into the empty seat next to Luca. Angelo looked at the faces of his family. No one looked at him, except for his father. Even his mother avoided his gaze. Angelo's heart felt like a stone in his chest.

"Is it true?" blurted out his Dad. "What Luca tells us—is it true?" His dark eyes bored into Angelo.

Angelo gazed at his father. Vittorio Tarallo was a tall, heavy-set man of sixty years, the black curls of his youth having been reduced to a scant layer of gray hair which he kept permanently trimmed as short as possible. He'd always been an imposing figure of a man, and age hadn't diminished that. And the one thing that Angelo had never been able to do successfully, was lie to his father.

Except now he was willing to try.

Angelo swallowed hard. "Is what true? You're going to have to give me a clue here, Dad."

"Don't try to deny it." Luca was sneering. "I saw you. You were holding hands with a bloke. Now, why would you be doing that? And let's not forget what I heard that queer bastard say to you." His lip curled up. "Go on, deny it."

"Luca! You will not use such language in this house." At last, some reaction from his mother. Vincente and Paolo stared at the table. Maria regarded him in silence, her eyes shining.

Luca glanced at his mother and his cheeks reddened.

"Is that enough of a clue for you?" his father said.

Angelo looked his father in the eye. He couldn't speak.

"Who is this man your brother speaks of?"

There was a lump of lead in Angelo's throat. "He's my... my boyfriend."

His father's face grew mottled. "No. No son of mine is a..a...*omosessuale*. It is not right. It is...it's..." His face darkened further. "*Esso è pervertito.*"

It didn't require an in-depth knowledge of Italian to work that one out.

"Dad, please, if you'll just listen to—"

"*NO!*" his father thundered. "It is you who will listen. I will not permit this....this...*infamita.*"

Another word from his childhood—*abomination.*

And right then Angelo had had enough of feeling scared. He got to his feet.

"Dad, it's who I am. I was born this way." His voice was as steady as he could make it. He held his chin high, and looked his father full in the face. "And Rick is important to me."

"Enough!" The word rang out. "Sit down, you...*finocchio.*"

Stunned into silence, Angelo dropped into his chair. No eyes met his, except for those of his father.

"This is what is going to happen," his father began. "You are never to see this Rick again. You will go to confession. You will find yourself a girlfriend— not that you need worry about that, as I have already sorted out a nice girl for you—and you will get married."

Angelo was already shaking his head, but his father held up his hand.

"If you choose not to follow my wishes, I will have no choice but to disown you. You will no longer be a member of this family."

Angelo stared at him in disbelief. He could hear

the rush of blood pounding through his head. He was about to speak when a new sound broke out into the stillness of his parents' dining room. His mother was weeping.

Anything he'd been on the verge of saying died in his throat. He couldn't stand to see her cry.

"Mum," he began, his throat tight.

She raised her head, her eyes wet, pleading with him. "*Mio figlio.*" The pain in her voice was like a lance through his heart. He looked at his sister, and saw the same desperation in her expression. He knew what they wanted him to do.

And God help him, he knew what he had to do.

"Okay," he said, his voice cracking. "I'll do what you say, sir." He wouldn't look at his father, even though he knew it was disrespectful. He gazed instead at his mother and sister. They said nothing, but the look in their eyes said plenty.

Angelo didn't hear the buzz of chatter that started up following his declaration. He barely felt his mother's arms around him as she hugged him so tightly against her. His brothers' cool looks bounced off him.

All he could see in his head was Rick. All he heard was Rick's sweet voice. All he felt was that warm, firm body as it had lain on top of him.

But you're giving all that up! The voice inside his head screamed at him.

What else can I do? he thought bitterly. All his life, it had been ingrained in him that children obey their parents. Okay, so he was old enough now to go against their wishes. When his father had issued his ultimatum, Angelo had been *this close* to defying him for the first time in his life. He would gladly have walked out that door and never come back—until his mother had started crying. The cynical part of his brain knew she was his father's trump card, but he couldn't help his reaction. That expression on her face. And the stricken look in Maria's eyes…

If I walk out now, I lose them.

It was a terrible choice to have to make. *NO ONE should be forced to choose like that. How the fuck do I choose between my family and the man who could mean more to me than any other guy I've ever known?*

And in the end it could only have gone one way.

His heart quaked. *What am I going to say to him?*

Angelo didn't have a clue how he'd gotten back to the studio. He couldn't remember a single thing about the journey. For the last three hours all he'd done was drink coffee and stare out of the window.

How the hell do I do this?

The question hammered into his brain. The one thing he was sure of was that it wouldn't be a face-to-face conversation. He couldn't take that. It was bad enough knowing he would be able to hear every nuance of pain in Rick's voice.

If it had been just a case of physical attraction, Angelo wouldn't have found this so difficult to contemplate. But it was more than that. It didn't matter that it had only been a matter of weeks since he and Rick had started dating. Something about Rick had called to him the first time he'd laid eyes on him back in January, but now that he'd gotten to know the man? Angelo wanted to crawl inside him, curl up and stay.

This is crazy. Stop torturing yourself.

He picked up his phone, only to put it back on the coffee table. Three times he tried, and three times it was beyond him to dial the number. He stared at it, willing himself to do what he knew needed to be done. With a sigh, he dialled Rick's number.

"Hey, how are you feeling?" Rick sounded really pleased to hear him. "I was going to leave off calling you 'til later, in case you were still feeling bad."

Angelo swallowed. "Rick, I…I need to talk to you."

Something in his voice must have gotten through. Rick's voice quietened. "What is it, babe?"

Babe. The simple endearment brought a lump to his throat. "This isn't going to be easy, but I figured it was best to do this now, before things got more serious."

Silence. Angelo could only imagine what was going through Rick's head in that moment. At last he spoke. "Go on." The cautious note in his voice tugged at Angelo's already stricken heart.

He took a deep breath. "Look, you and me? It isn't going to work, all right? I've been thinking about it all night, and I can't let it go on anymore. So…so I think it's best if we break it off."

He heard the hitch in Rick's breathing. "You're not serious. Are you?"

Angelo went for a lighter tone. "Oh come on, it's only been a couple of weeks. And it's not like we've even fucked yet, is it? We've shared a few dates and it was nice, but I think we both know it isn't going to go anywhere." He fought to hold back the tears as he dished out the blatant, horrible lies.

"What's this 'we' crap?" Rick yelled down the phone. "I thought things were going really well. I mean, I took you to meet my family, for God's sake. The first fucking guy I've ever taken there. I'd say that should tell you something." He fell silent for a moment. "Fuck, Angelo, why? Why are you doing this?" His voice broke.

Angelo couldn't tell him the truth. To do that would be disrespectful to his father, and that wasn't in his makeup. All he could do was lie through his teeth.

"I told you. It's just not working for me, that's all. So it's best to quit now."

"No, just... NO. What happened to '*I think we have something*'? And '*I want you in my life as a permanent feature, baby*'? Do you have any *fucking* idea how happy those words made me? Why do you think I can quote them from memory? *BECAUSE THEY WERE THAT FUCKING IMPORTANT TO ME, that's why!*"

Angelo winced. "Rick, I—"

"Oh, I think you've said all you need to say, don't you?" Rick's voice shook. "I just don't understand how you can do a complete one hundred and eighty degree turnaround, that's all. But at least you did it now, before things got more serious, as you said." His voice quavered. "But just so you know, before you disappear from my life? As far as I was concerned? Things were already pretty fucking serious." There was a moment's pause. Rick's breathing was harsh and rapid. "Well, fuck you, Angelo Tarallo." He hung up.

Angelo dropped the phone as if it were a live coal. Bile rose in his throat, and he swallowed hard. There was nothing in him but coffee. He drew his knees up and sat there on the couch, hugging them, his chin on his chest. For a moment, it felt as though time had stopped. He was hyper-aware of every little sound in the flat and the city beyond. Angelo was trapped in a bubble of time, caught in that moment of intense pain as the enormity of what he'd just done began to sink in.

And then the bubble burst. Angelo started crying.

Tears poured down his face as he wept for what he'd just lost. His body shook with the violence of his sobs as he let it all out: all the impotence he was feeling, the rage toward his father that he could never reveal, the total misery at the thought of never holding Rick in his arms again. He cried for what he'd never experience—making love with the most beautiful man ever to walk into his life.

Most of all, he cried at the thought of Rick, alone in his flat, trying to get his head around something that didn't make sense, because nothing about it was rational.

Angelo howled at the ceiling, his neck corded, until his voice was hoarse. He curled up into a tight ball on the couch and stared, eyes damp, at the window.

Oh baby, I'm sorry.

Rick threw the phone across the room. It landed on the carpeted floor by the kitchen door, its back cover shattering. He stared at it, unable to move.

What. The. Fuck. Happened?

He felt numb.

His brain tried to work through it, make some sense of it all. *Come on, how many times have you broken it off with a guy before it got too serious? You've been doing that for years. Only this time, someone's done it to you, that's all.*

He let that thought filter through. *Was* it the same thing?

"Fuck, no!" he shouted aloud. Walking away from a guy after fucking him once, maybe twice, was *not* the same thing. He never let *anyone* in, not like he'd let Angelo.

Maybe the guys you broke it off with felt just like you're feeling now. Remember Ben and Oli? Even they *were disappointed when you snuck out of their flat that morning. Ben said as much.*

He swallowed, his throat dry and constricted. *Was I such a bastard to all those guys? Is* that *what this is— payback?* He sat huddled on the couch, staring, unseeing. It wasn't sinking in.

That's because none of this makes ANY FUCKING SENSE!

And then the numbness wore off.

"How the fuck could you *do* this to me, Angelo?" He trembled as the full force of his grief hit him. "I let you in, you bastard! I fucking let you into my head, into my heart and then you go and do this— and I don't have a fucking clue *WHY!*"

He gulped, but the tears wouldn't be held back. They poured out of him, carrying him along on a wave of pain, until he was breathless, gasping as he tried to draw more air into his lungs. He got up from the couch, picked up his mug from the table and then slung it across the room where it smashed against the front door. He walked into his bedroom and stared down at the bed. He snatched up the pillows and hurled them at the mirror on his wardrobe door. Rick dropped face down onto the bed and screamed into the sheets, his whole body shaking uncontrollably as he gave vent to the emotions which coursed through him. Eventually, tears gave way to quiet sobs, leaving him shattered and confused.

He crawled under the duvet and pulled it up over his head. His body shook.

It hurts so much. God, just take it away. It hurts.

Eventually he figured God would listen.

Chapter Twelve

Life was a drunken haze. And that was exactly how Rick wanted it to stay. Because at least then the pain lessened a little.

Five days after Angelo had ruined his fucking life, and Rick still hadn't been to work. He couldn't face the thought of walking in there and having to tell Blake—or anyone, for that matter—what Angelo had done.

He gave his bedroom a cursory glance, noting the number of empty bottles in the bin beside his bed. That was easily fixed. He got out of bed and walked unsteadily into the kitchen to grab another bottle, before returning to the haven of his room. He dropped down onto the mattress, unscrewed the cap and took a long swig of its contents, before lying back against the pillows, staring at the ceiling.

Blake had tried calling. Will had tried calling. In the end Rick had switched off his phone and mentally told the outside world to go fuck itself. He was incommunicado. Out. Not Available. Eventually he reasoned, he'd have to go back, but at that moment the memory was still sharp.

His belly ached. Rick knew he'd have to eat something soon, but the lure of the duvet was too great. He put the bottle down on the bedside table and climbed back into bed, hauling the covers up over his head once more. He lay in his cozy cave, letting the wine blunt the edges of his pain some more.

He awoke from a doze to the sound of someone hammering on his front door.

"Just leave me the fuck alone," he grumbled as he tugged the covers around his ears. The duvet was a welcome weight. It felt like too much of an effort to get out of bed and answer it so he let whoever it was bang on the door until they ran out of steam and left.

Sometime later he awoke once more, emerging from beneath his covers to blink in the strong late afternoon sunshine that poured into his room. *I could've sworn I closed the bloody curtains.* He craned his neck to look at them and let out a yelp. Will stood beside his bed, hands in his pockets, staring down at him.

"What the fuck are you doing here?" Rick growled. Then it hit him. "And how in hell did you get in?" He sat up in bed and ran his fingers through his hair, raking his scalp.

"I got your landlord to let me in." Will looked distinctly unhappy. "Blake's been worried to death all week. It got so bad, he sent me round here to check you hadn't died or something."

"Well, you've seen me," Rick said, staring him in the face. "So you can report back that I'm very much alive. Bye, Will. Close the curtains on your way out." He sank back under the welcoming heaviness of his duvet, shutting Will out of sight.

Rick gasped as the duvet was dragged from his body. Will grabbed his arm and tugged him from the bed, only to heave him up over his shoulder.

"What the fuck're you doing?" He slapped Will hard on his jeans-clad arse, but Will ignored him and walked into the bathroom where he shoved Rick into the shower cubicle and turned on the water—cold. Rick screamed and tried to push his way past, but Will kicked off his shoes and climbed in with him, fully clothed, holding him under the water until they both shivered.

"When you've quite finished shouting," Will said through chattering teeth, "it's time for the drama queen to take a hike. I need Rick back." Rick leaned into him, body trembling. He felt the water grow warmer, as Will brought him back up to normal temperature and then switched off the water. Will grabbed a towel from the shelf and wrapped it around Rick, drying him off. Then he peeled off his sodden clothes and dried himself. He drew the towel around his hips, secured it, and then led Rick by the arm back into his bedroom. After pushing him insistently to sit on the bed, Will went to the chest of drawers and rifled through, taking out a clean pair of jeans, a T-shirt and a sweater. He threw them at Rick.

"Get dressed. And I don't suppose you've anything that will fit me, in the way of pants? I'm a good two inches taller than you."

Rick pointed to the bottom drawer. "There's a pair of jogging pants in there that were too long in the leg. I meant to return them to the shop, but I never got around to it." Without thinking he pulled on the clothes. Will found the pants and a baggy sweater, and got dressed. Rick sat back down on the bed and gazed with longing at the wine bottle. Will let out an exasperated huff and exited the bedroom. Rick could hear him banging cabinet doors in the kitchen, and then the opening and closing of the fridge.

"Do you know you have no food in this place whatsoever?" Will called out.

"Seeing as that would require me going shopping, and I haven't been out of the house since

Sunday, I'm not exactly surprised," Rick called back.

Will appeared in the bedroom doorway, holding out Rick's brown leather jacket and trainers. "Come on. I'm taking you someplace where I can feed you." He stared hard at Rick. "Today, Rick Wentworth. So move your arse."

Sighing, Rick got to his feet and followed Will out of the room. "You're not going to leave me alone until I do what you want, are you?"

He could hear the smile in Will's voice. "*Now* you're getting it."

"Feeling better?" Will asked him.

Rick pushed aside his empty plate and sat back in his seat. "Yeah." He had to admit, the Coffee Pot's All Day Breakfast was just what the doctor ordered. Then he remembered his manners. He gave Will a grateful smile. "Thanks, mate."

Will grinned. "Now that's my Rick." He poured out more coffee from the pot and handed Rick another cupful. "Drink this. I need you alert."

Rick drank eagerly. He drained the cup and then put it down with a sigh. "I feel miles better." He couldn't remember the last time he'd eaten.

Will leaned forward, hands wrapped around his coffee cup. "Okay, suppose you tell me what the hell is going on."

Rick took a breath and then let it all come tumbling out. Will listened intently, his face growing longer as Rick went on. Finally Rick stopped. It still hurt like hell, but at least he'd shared it with someone.

"And you have no idea why he dumped you?"

Rick shook his head. "I spent the first part of the week going over everything in my head, over and over, until I felt like I was going crazy. I still don't have a clue. After that, I stopped trying to analyse it to death and just got drunk." His stomach rolled. Yeah, it still hurt.

Will looked saddened. "Aw, cutie, I'm so sorry. I know you had high hopes of this one lasting."

"You're not going to say, 'I told you so', are you?" Rick inquired. "Because if so, you can leave now. I don't need that right now." He met Will's gaze with a forthright stare. *Amazing how a simple thing like food restores the balance.*

"I wouldn't dream of it," Will replied earnestly. "Rick, I know this is painful. I remember how I felt when Blake and I split because of that bitch Melissa. But I do need you to pull yourself together, because right now, your work needs you. Blake needs you." He twisted his engagement ring nervously on his finger.

Rick lowered his gaze to the tabletop with its red-and-white checked tablecloth. He knew it had to come, sooner or later. Maybe it was past the time for wallowing in self-pity, especially if he was letting his colleagues down. He listened to the babble of voices around him, all happily oblivious to what was going on in his head. Then he took one more look at Will's unhappy expression.

"I'll go back to work," he said at last.

The look of relief on Will's face was heart-lifting. "Thank you," he said, reaching across the table to take Rick's hand in his.

Rick smiled, even though it was the last thing he felt like doing.

There's going to come a day when it doesn't hurt so much,

he told himself.

He hoped.

"Tell me again what I pay you for. Because from where I'm standing, it isn't for shoddy workmanship. And especially not after you missed the deadline."

Angelo held the phone away from his ear as the strident voice drilled through his head. When everything grew quieter, he returned to the call. "I'm sorry, Mr. Entwistle, I'll get that sorted out for you as quickly as possible." He sighed internally. He didn't need this shit.

Mr. Entwistle's voice softened. "What's going on, Angelo? I've never known you to be like this. Careless mistakes, missed deadlines.... Is there something going on that I need to know about?"

Angelo hastened to reassure his client. "Nothing that will jeopardize the opening of the bar, I assure you. I'll get onto it right away. Don't worry, you'll open on time." *Even if I have to work until midnight every night to catch up.* He forced himself to sound confident.

Apparently it worked. "That's all I needed to know," Bernard Entwistle said. Angelo could hear the relief in his voice. "I'll see you soon, then?"

He reassured his client once more and then hung up, putting his phone back into his jeans pocket. He sank down onto the stool in front of his workbench and leaned over, laying his head on his folded arms.

You can't keep on like this. At this rate you're going to start losing clients.

God, he was a mess. It was four weeks since

he'd made the mistake of listening to his father and had fucked up his life. Four long, lonely weeks. His stomach clenched.

Fuck, Rick, I miss you.

He kept waiting for the pain to lessen, but it seemed that with each passing day, the memories grew more vivid. He dreamed of Rick. He fantasized about Rick, to the point where he'd get into bed each night and close his eyes, hoping to see Rick in his dreams where they could be together. But such thoughts carried their own toll. His work was suffering, and he couldn't allow that to happen. This latest fiasco involved the opening of a new bar in Soho. The interior was heavy with carved wood, giving it a Gothic feel. And if he brought this off, it would mean more clients.

So for God's sake, get your shit together, he told himself sternly.

The doorbell to the studio rang, startling Angelo from his reveries. He walked across to open the door and then stiffened. Maria stood outside, carrying a shopping bag over her arm.

"Did you want something?" he asked her. She hadn't been in touch since the family meeting, and Angelo had felt no inclination to call. The less time he spent around his family, the better.

Maria's face fell. She held out her bag. "I brought us some lunch. I figured it was time I called round to see if you were okay." She fingered the lace collar of her blouse.

He looked closely at her. Her eyes were puffy and there were dark circles underneath them. He sighed heavily. "Come on in." He stood aside to let her enter.

Maria walked through the studio, gazing at the projects which covered his work benches. She stopped by one bench where he'd covered up his work with a red cloth. "What's under here?"

"Something I'm working on," he said hastily, guiding her toward the stairs which led up to his flat. "You want to go eat upstairs?"

Maria shook her head. "I like it fine down here. I love the smell of wood and linseed oil." She smiled. "But some plates would be good."

Reluctantly he left her in the studio while he raced up the stairs, two at a time, to his flat. When he returned a minute or so later with two plates and cutlery, his heart gave a jolt. She'd lifted off the red cloth and was staring at the carved head below it. "What kind of wood is this?" she asked.

His heart began to beat more normally at the simple question. "Lime wood," he replied. "It's good for carving busts and intricate stuff like that because it's softer."

She nodded and then lifted her head to look directly at him. "This is him, isn't it?"

Angelo caught his breath. He'd started carving Rick's likeness from memory about three weeks ago, working on it when the need to think of him grew most acute. Somehow it eased his pain.

"Yes, that's Rick."

To his surprise, Maria picked up her stool and moved it to the work bench where the bust stood. She placed her bag on the table and withdrew two store-bought boxes of salad.

Angelo couldn't help his chuckle. "I see Mum still hasn't managed to teach you how to cook yet."

Maria rolled her eyes. "Don't you start. She still

complains about the time instant mashed potato mysteriously turned into potato soup." She snorted. "Cookery and I will never be on speaking terms."

And just like that the tension between them melted.

"How are you?" she asked. Her eyes scanned his face.

Angelo opened his salad and took a forkful of cucumber, tomatoes and roast chicken. He chewed slowly, swallowed and then looked at her. "I've been better," he said softly. Dad had rung three nights ago. It seemed he was trying to set Angelo up on a date with Luisa Pascuale, the daughter of a business associate who was also from an old Sicilian family. There was nothing set in stone as yet, but it would only be a matter of time.

Maria ate a few mouthfuls of salad, then she put down her fork. She stroked a finger over the smooth grain of the wood. "Tell me about him."

Angelo gave a start. "About Rick?" She nodded. "Why?" It seemed to him to be a pointless—and painful—exercise.

"Humour me," she demanded.

Angelo turned the bust slowly until he gazed at the face which was burned into his memory. He told her about seeing Rick for the first time at Heaven. He even told her about rescuing him from Julian.

Her eyes went wide. "My brother, the hero."

Angelo's cheeks heated up. He told her what kind of man Rick was. She listened intently. He'd expected some comments about Rick, but she said nothing. When he'd finally run out of things to say, she regarded him thoughtfully.

"There's someone I'd like you to talk to."

Angelo frowned. "Who?"

Maria shrugged. "Just a friend of mine. His name's Franco."

Angelo quirked an eyebrow. "Why would I want to talk to this friend of yours?"

She smiled enigmatically. "Like I said before, humour me." And with that, she went back to her lunch.

They ate in comfortable silence. Occasionally Angelo would catch her gazing at Rick's bust.

What are you up to?

Then he pushed the thought from his mind. There was already way too much going on his head, he didn't need more. He reasoned that whatever was on her mind, he'd find out soon enough. Besides, he had other things to think about.

Like a date with Luisa Pascuale.

Chapter Thirteen

April was on its way out, Spring was well and truly sprung and Rick was getting his act together, slowly but surely.

It had been five weeks or so since Will had dragged him, kicking and screaming, back into Trinity Publishing. Okay, so maybe that was a slight exaggeration. There were still days—'*black dog days*', Rick called them,. after something he'd read about Winston Churchill—when he would feel so low, it required a major effort to haul his arse out of bed, but Rick persevered. The change in season helped lift his spirits, and he looked forward to the coming of summer. As the cooler weather made its exit, Rick tried to slough off the last of the Angelo blues. He kept telling himself that he was getting over the handsome, dark-eyed gentleman who had made his home in Rick's heart—before ripping it apart.

His colleagues had been absolutely brilliant. The last thing he'd wanted was for them to be whispering in corners about what could possibly have happened, so that first day back, he'd waited until the end of Blake's team meeting, and then he'd addressed them all. Speaking calmly and quietly, he'd told them everything that had transpired. When he'd finished, there was a stunned silence. Ed had sworn under his breath, and then lapsed into silence once more. Lizzie had got up from her chair, walked over to where Rick was sitting and wrapped her arms around him, hugging him tightly. Beth had been next, and then the guys on the team had patted him on the back or the arm. Everyone had let him know, in their own way, that they supported him. Blake's look of approval had warmed him inside. And from that day on, although no one had spoken of it again, he'd been conscious of his team's continued support.

Monday morning, Rick was working on the upcoming Easter sale event when his phone rang. He glanced at the screen and froze. It was Julian. His fingers seemed to react faster than his brain—he hit Decline in an instant. To his dismay, his heart was beating rapidly. He could only stare at the screen, struggling to remain calm. It had taken a while, but eventually his heartbeat returned to normal.

The next day, the local florist delivered a bouquet of roses, lilies and freesia. Their delicate perfume had everyone sniffing the air appreciatively as Karen carried them through the corridor. Rick watched her walk toward him and froze when she halted in front of him, proudly holding out the fragrant flowers.

"Someone sent me flowers? Well, there's a first time for everything," he mused. As he took them from Karen, for one illogical moment he thought that maybe Angelo had…. Then he dismissed it. He didn't need to torture himself like that. He walked into his office, deposited them on his desk and opened the envelope. His jaw dropped.

Forgive me. Julian X

He has to be fucking kidding! Rick tore up the card and walked into Beth's office with the flowers. She stared at them with wide eyes.

"Don't ask me where they came from, but I'd consider it a great favour if you'd take these off my hands." Rick smiled. "I figure they should go to someone who would get some pleasure from them."

Beth smiled and kissed him on the cheek. "Got it—and thanks, Rick."

Rick walked back into his office and closed the door. He sat down at his desk and rubbed his temples. What the fuck was Julian playing at?

It figures. I just about get some semblance of normality back into my life, and now this.

When a courier turned up two days later, looking for Rick, bearing chocolates and champagne, Rick's stomach churned and he fought the desire to run into the nearest bathroom and throw up. The message sent shivers down his spine.

We need to talk. Please. Julian X

And then the calls began.

The first time Karen put the call through, she didn't tell him who the caller was. The moment he heard Julian's voice, Rick slammed the phone down so fast, he thought he'd broken it. He left his office, shaking, and walked into the reception area to tell Karen exactly who had called and why she wasn't to put him through again. When he'd finished speaking, Karen was white-faced. Rick went straight into the men's room and threw up.

But it didn't end there. During the course of the next week, Julian tried to speak with him eight or nine times. And then the texts started up.

Please - I need to talk to you.

Please - give me a chance.

One more chance, please?

By the tenth call and the umpteenth text, Rick

had had enough. He closed his office door and walked over to his window. Leaning his head against the glass, he took a minute to compose himself, and then got out his phone and dialled.

"Oh God, finally." Julian sounded overjoyed. "I was beginning to think I'd never get to speak with you again."

"What do you want, Julian?" Rick kept his voice level, despite the tremors running through him.

"Rick, I am so, so sorry. I don't know what came over me that night."

Rick couldn't believe this. "You're sorry? You were inches away from *raping* me and you're *sorry*?"

He heard the sharp intake of breath. "Rape? Oh God—is *that* what you think I was doing?" Julian *sounded* shocked, Rick gave him that much. "I thought you might get off on the whole 'taken by force' bit. I never thought you'd take it seriously."

That stopped Rick in his tracks. *Did I overact? Did I read that whole situation wrong?* His mind raced, trying to go back and analyse everything little thing Julian had said or done. *Did I turn myself into a victim here?*

"Oh God, Rick. What you must have gone through, thinking I'd done that to you." Julian's voice softened. "Please, baby, can we meet up? Just for coffee? I think we need to talk."

Rick was having a serious case of déjà vu. *Where have I heard these words before?*

"What do you say, Rick?" Julian's tone was coaxing. "Maybe we should get together, see if we can't come back from this." His voice dropped low. "Especially as I thought it was leading somewhere."

Rick was being carried along by the silky tone of Julian's voice. *At least someone wants me*, he thought. He

thought about the prospect of meeting Julian again.
Can I do this?

"Rick? Are you still there?"

Rick gathered his thoughts. "Yeah, I'm still here." He still didn't know what to say.

Julian forged ahead. "We could meet in Covent Garden, if you like. There's a great little coffee shop near the theatre. It's quiet, cozy..." There was that coaxing tone again. "Come on, Rick, you could probably do with a good chat. And it's not like you have anyone right now."

Rick froze. "What?"

"Aw, it's okay, babe. I heard that hairy, spaghetti-eating greaseball is leaving you alone these days."

It took Rick a few seconds to breathe normally. Then a moment more to frame exactly what he wanted to say.

"One, I don't know how the *fuck* you know that, but it's none of your *fucking* business what went on between Angelo and me. Two, how *dare* you talk about someone like that!" Rick was gathering speed. "It only goes to show me what a bigoted prick you really are. And three... I should be grateful that you *are* such a prick, because at least it's brought me to my senses. To think I was actually letting you talk me into seeing you again. God, you must take me for a real mug." He breathed deeply. "So you can take your insults and shove it. Don't call me again. Don't send me gifts. I want nothing whatsoever to do with you. And I hope the next guy you try that whole 'taken by force' routine on, has more guts than I did and reports you to the police."

Julian gasped. "Rick, what—"

"One last thing, Julian. Angelo Tarallo is ten times the man you'll ever be. Just so you know." He disconnected the call and sat back, shaking. Adrenaline pumped through his system. *I said no to the son of a bitch. And bloody hell, that felt good.*

And just like that, his thoughts went to Angelo.

What we had was special. Why the hell did you throw it away?

It was like a wound had opened up, raw and weeping.

No. Not over Angelo. Not even close.

Angelo lovingly rubbed linseed oil into the finished bust. Rick's face stared back at him, the likeness so true it hurt to look at him. Angelo still marvelled that his hands had done this. It was easily the best carving he'd ever worked on. He traced the line of Rick's eyebrow and then stroked his cheek.

"Still miss you, babe," he whispered.

The doorbell to the studio buzzed. Angelo wiped his hands on a soft cloth and went to answer it. Maria stood in the street, along with a guy possibly in his late thirties, dressed in a black leather jacket and jeans. Maria carried a linen bag.

"Hi, can we come in?"

Angelo stepped aside. He kissed Maria on the cheek and then regarded Maria's friend. "Who's this, sis?"

"Remember I said I had someone I wanted you to meet? This is Franco."

Angelo shook Franco's hand and then gave him a speculative glance. "Look, Franco, I don't want to seem rude, but I know nothing about you, or why Maria has brought you to meet me."

Franco glanced around the studio with its workbenches, tools and wooden stools. "Is there somewhere we can go to sit and talk more comfortably?"

Angelo frowned. "I'm sorry, I seem to have forgotten my manners. Come upstairs." He led them to the staircase and up to his flat. Once inside, he pointed them in the direction of the lounge and asked them to sit.

"Actually, Franco is going to sit and talk," Maria said with a twinkle in her eye. "*I* am going to make lunch for the three of us."

Angelo looked at her for a minute and then did a visible gulp. He glanced at Franco. "Be afraid, Franco. Be very afraid."

Franco guffawed and Maria huffed as she flounced into the kitchen. Angelo took a seat on the couch next to Franco. He bit the inside of his cheek. "Okay, so what is this about?" He was intrigued by his guest.

Franco relaxed into the couch and undid his jacket. "I think it's only fair to warn you that your sister and I have talked a great deal about your present situation."

Angelo became very still. "Situation?" he echoed.

Franco nodded. "Your father's ultimatum, your decision, your boyfriend Rick…."

"Not my boyfriend anymore," Angelo said softly. The expression of sympathy which flickered across Franco's face made him warm to his mystery guest.

"Tell me about Rick. What was he like?" Franco's gaze was fixed on him.

Angelo smiled. "Rick was...*is* funny." He shook his head. "I'm sorry. He may be out of my life but I can't bring myself to talk about him in the past tense. That would feel too much like he'd... died." Franco nodded slowly and Angelo resumed. "He's very generous. He's compassionate. He adores his family." He talked quietly for several minutes more, sharing what he'd learned about Rick from their conversations. Franco listened, never interrupting. When Angelo had finished, Franco studied him intently for a minute.

"You care a great deal for him."

Angelo swallowed. He couldn't speak for a moment.

"Okay," Franco began slowly, "now tell me about your father. For instance, tell me how you feel about his ultimatum."

Angelo sighed. "What is there to tell? He's my father. I have to do what he says."

Franco sat up at that part. "Angelo, God created us with the choice to make our own paths. 'Honour thy father and thy mother' doesn't mean you live your life according to their rules. And 'honour' doesn't translate as 'obey'. Besides, you're a grown man." He peered intently at Angelo. "God gave us the gift of His grace and free will."

Angelo was definitely intrigued. "You seem very knowledgeable about such matters."

Franco grinned. "I should be—I'm a priest. Albeit an incognito one right now."

Angelo's mouth fell open.

Franco smiled, leaned forward and took hold of his hand. "*All* God's children are loved, Angelo." His eyes sparkled. "Even those children who are gay."

Angelo's chest tightened. "But...it's a mortal sin." He was dimly aware of noises emanating from the kitchen.

Franco shook his head and frowned. "Mortal sin? No. A sin? Perhaps." He sighed heavily. "There are some theologians who don't believe the Bible's teachings on this have been done correctly."

Now it was Angelo's turn to straighten. He tilted his head to one side. "Are you gay?"

Franco met his gaze with a calm expression. "If I am gay or not doesn't matter. I'm celibate. I take my vows seriously."

Heat rose to Angelo's cheeks.

Franco released Angelo's hand and folded his arms across his chest. He gazed at him with clear green eyes. "Angelo, you have two choices. You obey your father and take a wife—and not only will *you* be miserable, so will she, because you'll never love her as a man should love his wife." He smiled. "*Or* you decide for yourself who you are going to gift your heart to, and see that love returned." There was a look of such understanding in Franco's eyes that Angelo's throat tightened. "Okay, it will alienate you from your family, but that may change. They may come to agree. You never know. 'Blood is thicker than water' is the age-old saying." He tilted his head. "Do you think they will stay that way forever?" He grasped Angelo's hand once more and held it firmly. "You have to ask yourself what is it you want."

"That's a very good question," Maria said as she entered the lounge with a tray bearing three bowls of steaming soup, and a plate with chunks of fresh bread. She put down the tray on the coffee table and came across to hug Angelo. She pressed her cheek against his. "Whatever you decide, *fratello mio*," she whispered, "I will always love you."

He hugged her tightly. Maria handed them their bowls of soups and then sank into the armchair with her own. They ate in silence. Angelo's thoughts were in a whirl as he digested both the soup and Franco's wise words.

When it was time for his guests to leave, Angelo saw them to his door and waved them off. He looked toward Rick's bust and his heart gave a jolt as he gazed on that face which had emerged out of the wood. He looked at his hands. God had given him a talent to create beauty. And then he thought about Franco telling him all God's children were loved. One phrase stuck in his mind.

You decide for yourself who you are going to gift your heart to, and see that love returned.

That one word sent a wave of warmth rolling through him, filling him completely.

Love.

It was Friday afternoon, two days after Maris and Franco's visit, and Angelo pushed open the glass door which led to Trinity Publishing. He approached the reception desk where a kindly-faced woman sat peering at a computer screen. She glanced up at him and smiled.

"Can I help you?"

Angelo gave her his most winning smile. "I'd like to see Rick Wentworth, please. If he's available." Her name tag read Karen.

As she reached for her phone, a guy Angelo's height but much stockier strolled through the reception area. He grinned at Karen as he placed a folder on her desk. "Blake asked me ter drop this off for yer, with 'is apologies. Seems he walked off with it by mistake this mornin'."

Karen clasped the handset to her chest and tut-tutted. "He had me looking *everywhere* for that!" She gave the man a beaming smile. "Thanks, Ed." She peered at Angelo. "What name shall I give?"

"Angelo Tarallo." His heart pounded as he thought of seeing Rick once more. *Though how he's going to feel about seeing* me *remains to be seen.*

Ed stiffened. "Angelo Tarallo?"

Angelo jerked his head at the sharp edge to his voice. "Er, yes?"

Ed walked up to him and got right in his face. "You've got a bleedin' nerve, mate, showin' up 'ere after that stunt you pulled."

Oh fuck. Angelo stood up straight. "If I could just see Rick, I—"

"*See* Rick? I'm not lettin' you within three fuckin' *feet* of him!" Ed yelled. "Now sling yer 'ook!"

Angelo gritted his teeth. "I'm going nowhere until I've seen Rick."

"Then yer gonna be waitin' a bleedin' long time because 'ell will freeze over 'fore I let you anywhere near 'im. You've already 'urt 'im enough." Ed's cheeks were bright red, the muscles in his upper arms tensed and his fists clenched. His face was inches away from Angelo's. But Angelo stood firm.

Footsteps heralded the approach of three or four startled people.

"What the hell is going on here?"

A guy in a dark blue suit, with black hair and the bluest eyes Angelo had ever seen strode across to them. Ed didn't move an inch.

"Ed, back off, now."

Ed narrowed his lips and took a couple of steps back. "This is Angelo, boss." He sneered as if the name itself carried a foul odour.

This had to be Blake Davis. "Even if he was the Devil himself, you do *not* carry out a shouting match with him, not in this building. Is that clear?" Blake said, his voice low but firm. "Now back…away."

Ed moved away with reluctance and joined the others who watched the scene with wide eyes. Blake turned to Angelo.

"My apologies, Mr. Tarallo, for my office manager's behaviour." He extended a hand. "I'm Blake Davis, owner of Trinity Publishing."

As Angelo took the proffered hand, Rick appeared as he dashed around the corner and came to a halt, open-mouthed, when he caught sight of Angelo. The colour slid from his face.

They regarded each other in silence, until Blake broke the spell, clearing his throat.

"Rick, why don't you take Angelo into the conference room and find out why he's here. Everyone else, back to work." Blake glanced at Ed who stood red-faced a few feet away. "Ed, my office. Now." He gave Ed a grim smile and then strode off, Ed trudging in his wake.

Angelo watched the little crowd of onlookers disperse, ripples of conversation trailing behind them as they walked away, until only he and Rick remained.

Rick seemed to have recovered a little from his shock. He pulled himself up to his full height and looked Angelo in the eye. "You'd better come with me." He turned on his heel and walked off along the corridor.

Angelo followed, his heart sinking. The positive thoughts which had swept him all the way to Rick's office on a tide of optimism, had deserted him, leaving him floundering.

This is not going to be good.

Chapter Fourteen

Rick closed the door to the conference room behind him and turned to face Angelo, his heart hammering. Angelo stood by the table, absolutely still.

"Why are you here?" Rick asked, swallowing hard. God, it hurt to look at him. It might have been weeks since he'd laid eyes on Angelo, but it felt like it was yesterday, the ache inside him just as acute.

"I needed to talk to you."

Rick frowned. "The last time you uttered those words, you ended the conversation by dumping me." He stayed where he was.

Angelo apparently had other plans. He walked toward Rick, eyes trained on him. "I am so sorry for hurting you the way I did. I know it was cruel, but at the time I couldn't see any way out."

"At the time?" For some reason those three words sparked in Rick's brain. "Are you saying something's changed?" He held his breath. In his head he was willing Angelo to continue. *Go on, explain it. For God's sake, let me in on it.* It was the not knowing that had haunted him during the last month or so.

Angelo held out his hand. "Please, Rick, sit down with me. Hear me out."

Rick stared at his outstretched hand for a moment before stepping forward and slipping his into it. A look of relief etched itself on Angelo's face. He led them to the table and they both sat, chairs turned toward each other. Angelo didn't let go of that hand.

Rick listened, his heart sinking, as Angelo told

him about the family meeting he'd been summoned to, and his father's ultimatum. He thought about how much pain Angelo must have been in. Whichever way he turned, he lost. *Would I have made the same decision, faced with those choices?* For the life of him, Rick didn't know. But at least he realized why Angelo had walked away from him.

It still doesn't explain why he's just walked back, however.

"I don't understand," Rick exclaimed. "Why are you here? Has your father changed his mind?" He couldn't understand how a parent could profess to love their child and then hurt them like that.

Angelo shook his head. "I'm here because of you. I have to be where you are."

Rick froze. "What are you saying?" He was acutely aware of his heartbeat, pounding in his ears.

Angelo smiled and suddenly his face was transformed as if it were alight from within. "I'm saying that I need to follow my heart and not my head."

Rick tried to get his brain around it. "But if you do that, you'll lose your family. Your mum, your sister." The enormity of Angelo's new direction began to dawn on him.

"Maybe," Angelo said, shrugging his shoulders. "Time will tell." Rick didn't miss the flash of pain in his eyes.

Rick couldn't let him do it. "Angelo, you've only known me for such a short time. How can you choose me over your family? Because that *is* what you're doing, isn't it?" *He chose...me.* The tight fist around his heart eased.

"Oh yes," Angelo said simply. "And I'm doing it

because the alternative is unthinkable." He grasped Rick's other hand and stared him in the face. "Let me tell you a story. There I was, standing at the bar in Heaven, the end of the first week in January, when this simply beautiful bloke caught my eye. He was drop-dead gorgeous, and I couldn't take my eyes off him. The way he moved, lost in the music, so sexy and yet seemingly unaware of the admiring glances of the men around him. I wanted to get to know him. A dance with him would have been enough. But I missed my chance. Another guy got there first, one Julian Emerson."

Rick stared at him. "Oh my God," he said softly.

Angelo nodded, never taking his eyes off Rick. "I got worried. I'd heard rumours around the place, you see. So I decided to watch out for my beautiful guy, hoping that if he came back and anything *did* happen, I'd be there for him, to protect him."

Realization dawned. "Oh hell. You didn't just happen to be in that bathroom, did you? You were worried about me, looking out for me."

Angelo smiled. "You needed looking after."

Rick was reeling. But Angelo wasn't finished.

"And then, of course, I got to know the man behind the beautiful exterior. Know what I found out?" His eyes lit up. "That the interior was just as beautiful. The more time I spent around you, the more I discovered about you." He swallowed. "A day doesn't go by when I don't think about you. I wake up, you're in my thoughts. I close my eyes, you're there, in my head. I don't give a damn that I only saw you for the first time just over four months ago. I only know that this is right. This...fits." He squeezed Rick's hands. "*This* is meant to be. I'm just sorry we had to go through so much pain in order for me to find that out."

Rick could only stare at him.

Angelo took a breath. "So this is me sitting here, asking my beautiful man to forgive me for not seeing that what we had was too precious to walk away from. To give me—give *us*—another chance. And this time, I promise, I'll hold on to what we have, and fight anyone who tries to take that away from us."

Tears prickled the inside of Rick's eyelids. He blinked hard, several times, determined not to lose it.

Angelo reached into his jacket pocket. "I have a gift for you. Except now that I'm here, it seems silly."

Rick gave a slow smile. "A gift?" He gave an involuntary little bounce on the chair. "What is it?"

Angelo let out a wry chuckle. "You big kid. Now that I think about it, this is the perfect gift. Put out your hands and close your eyes."

Rick obeyed, grinning like an idiot. He felt Angelo place something hard and slender in his cupped palms. He frowned. *What the hell?*

"Okay, you can open your eyes now."

Rick opened his eyes eagerly and stared down at…. His jaw dropped.

"You bought me a sonic screwdriver?" The words came out as a squeal. He pressed a button on the side. The tip glowed blue and there was the sound he always associated with Doctor Who's famous tool. "Oh bloody hell, Angelo. This is *perfect!*" The thought that had gone into the gift was staggering.

Just then the door opened and Ed stuck his head around. "Is everyfin' all right in 'ere?" Rick could see the barely held-in-check hostility in his glance at Angelo.

"Ed, everything's just fine," he said quickly. He beamed. Everything was more than fine.

He watched Ed's incredulous expression melt away. "Yeah?"

Rick was sure his face was glowing. "Oh yeah."

Ed looked across at Angelo and gave him a quick nod, before winking at Rick. "I'll just leave yer both to it, then." Then he withdrew.

Angelo was staring at him. "Does this mean—"

Rick stopped his words with a sweet, chaste kiss. He felt Angelo stiffen. Seconds later Angelo's hands cupped his face tenderly and the kiss continued, slow and perfect. *God, I've missed his kisses.* He leaned into Angelo, wanting more, needing more.

The sound of a cough had them breaking apart. Blake stood in the doorway, his eyes bright with amusement. He pointed at Rick.

"You're finishing early today. Like…now." He grinned and then turned to Angelo. "And you're going to take him home." He winked.

Rick couldn't stop smiling. "Yes, sir."

Blake shook his head and stepped out into the corridor. Rick could hear him chuckling.

He got to his feet and took Angelo's hand in his. "You heard what the man said. Take me home."

Angelo's face shone. "With pleasure."

The journey home was quiet. Rick was trying to take in everything Angelo had said, but he kept coming back to that one overwhelming fact. Angelo had chosen *him*. Whatever else happened between them, he would always remember that. The pain he'd suffered felt like a distant memory, indistinct, fuzzy even. To know that Angelo had weighed the prospect of a possible future with Rick against the risk of alienating his family, maybe losing them from his life altogether, and *still* had chosen Rick... Fuck, that was heady. It swept away any lingering doubts about the man at his side.

And that was exactly where Rick wanted him to stay.

For as long as we both shall live. Isn't that *how it goes?* The thought sent a shiver rippling through him

Angelo said nothing, but there was a calm which radiated from him, a peace which flowed out of him, unlike anything Rick had ever sensed before. He felt it settle over him, like a fine, warm blanket, soft against his skin.

And then it began, a need which vibrated through him, a yearning which built slowly, pulling him along toward a point in the distance which grew brighter, sharper, more vibrant as it got closer. Rick knew what was coming. Hell, he was praying for it. They'd waited long enough.

Angelo pulled into the parking bay behind Rick's block and switched off the engine. Before Rick could get out, Angelo was there, holding the door for him, holding out a hand for him. Rick took the proffered hand and allowed Angelo to lead him, unhurried, into the building. They held hands in the elevator, not breaking the connection once. Rick was hyper-aware of the sound of Angelo's breathing, slow and measured. It was as if time had slowed down, making him sensitive to the electrical current which sparked and crackled as they drew closer.

It's coming. I can feel it. And he feels it too.

The anticipation was exquisite.

Once inside the flat, Rick's nerves set in. He decided to try and slow things down. There was no rush, after all. He took off his leather jacket and went into the kitchen to see if he had a bottle of wine in the fridge. Angelo leaned against the door jamb, watching him. Even without turning around, Rick could feel those eyes on him, that gaze slowly traveling the length of his body. A frisson of excitement danced up and down his spine.

"What are you looking for?" Angelo asked him.

"Some wine." He withdrew a bottle of white wine from the fridge door, and then two glasses from the cabinet. Angelo followed him back into the lounge and then surprised him by taking the items from him and placing them on the coffee table.

"We don't need wine," Angelo said quietly. Then Rick was in his arms, and *oh yes, there* is *a God*, because finally, in the middle of his lounge, Angelo Tarallo was kissing him, long, slow kisses that seemed to go on and on, until Rick moaned hungrily. Angelo stroked languidly up and down his back, before taking hold of his arse and pulling him tight against that firm body.

"Oh God, don't stop," Rick groaned into his mouth.

"Not God—Angelo." The chuckle reverberated through him.

"Smart arse," Rick growled as Angelo freed his mouth, only to kiss down his neck, sucking at the skin. Rick rolled his head back with a low cry when Angelo sucked hard. *There's going to be a love bite there.* He shuddered at the thought of Angelo marking him.

Angelo cupped Rick's chin and looked at him,

those dark eyes thoughtful. "Remember the last night we spent together, before my Dad decided to ruin my life?"

Rick nodded, his cheeks on fire with the memory of that orgasm.

"Do you remember what you said?"

And suddenly Rick's whole body was on fire. "Yes," he whispered. He took another breath and locked eyes with Angelo. "I said I wanted the real thing."

Angelo nodded slowly. His coal-black eyes glowed like burnished metal. "Then why don't you show me your bedroom, and we'll see what the real thing feels like."

Without a word Rick led him by the hand into his bedroom and closed the door behind them. He watched as Angelo glanced around the room with a smile.

"Very nice," he said, pointing to the mirror above the padded headboard of the bed. He went over to the bed and pulled back the covers. Rick watched him, heart racing. Angelo straightened and beckoned to Rick, his finger crooked.

"Come here." Angelo's voice was husky.

Rick walked over to him and Angelo enfolded him in those strong arms, kissing him deeply. Rick closed his eyes and lost himself in the heady kiss.

I could drown in his kisses.

He shivered as Angelo began to undress him, fingers moving deliberately as they stripped away his clothing. When Rick reached for Angelo's shirt buttons, Angelo nodded, eyes bright. Both of them trembled. Rick gazed at the chest he'd only seen via a webcam. He ran his fingers through the mat of black hair which covered his pecs and then moved lower down the fuzzy belly. Angelo unfastened his jeans and pushed them past his hips, revealing a pad of jet black curls at the base of his already filling cock, and thighs covered with a fine layer of down.

Rick found his body responding. Who knew hair could be so fucking sexy?

He stroked the length of Angelo's hard dick. "It's even better looking in real life," he told Angelo with a smile. Angelo closed his eyes and bit his lip as Rick did nothing more than stroke him, keeping the touch light.

Angelo shuddered. "Let's get rid of the clothes, okay? I need to touch you."

Rick was all for that.

Angelo stepped from his jeans and then reached for Rick's pants. He slipped his hands under the waistband to push them down, slowly, his eyes feasting on Rick's emerging nude form. His briefs swelled as his dick hardened, pre-come already dampening the fabric. Angelo knelt before him and kissed the moist spot, before edging his fingers under the briefs to grasp the firm flesh of his shaft. Rick shuddered to feel Angelo's hand finally on him, his long fingers wrapping around his dick, stroking it, teasing yet more shivers from him.

Angelo looked up at him and smiled. "Want to see you," he said, his voice thick with desire as he lowered the briefs and removed both them and the pants. He pulled off Rick's socks and there he was, naked, cock rising to meet those warm lips which kissed the wet tip, pulling a whimper from him. He wanted—no, *needed*—Angelo's mouth on him, but Angelo wasn't following the script. As Angelo rose to his feet, ignoring Rick's waving dick which was clearly *begging* for attention, Rick let out another whimper.

Angelo didn't chuckle at the plaintive sound. He pushed Rick toward the bed and then kept on pushing until Rick was lying on his back, head cradled by his pillows. Angelo stretched out beside Rick and gazed down at him, his head movement slow and deliberate as he surveyed every inch of him. Rick could feel the weight of Angelo's cock against his thigh, felt its warmth as Angelo rocked his hips and let it slide over him.

Angelo leaned over and kissed him, lips brushing softly over Rick's. Their eyes met. Rick held his breath as Angelo trailed his hand over Rick's chest, fingertips rubbing over his nipples, making him squirm. The lack of talk only added to the heady atmosphere which pervaded the room. Angelo was focused on him intently, watching each reaction as he stroked and caressed Rick's body. When he ran his fingers through Rick's pubic bush to circle the base of his cock, Rick let out a little gasp and arched up off the bed. Angelo's eyes gleamed.

He rolled onto his back, stuffed pillows under his head and tugged Rick astride him, pulling him forward until Rick straddled his upper chest, his dick jutting toward Angelo's waiting mouth. Rick groaned as Angelo placed his hands on Rick's arse and propelled him forward, craning his neck to take the head of his cock into hot, wet heat. Rick pushed the top of his head into the padded headboard, staring down at the sight of his dick disappearing into Angelo's mouth, only to re-emerge gleaming wet. Angelo stared up at him as he licked and sucked his glistening shaft. Rick watched, mesmerized, as Angelo took him deeper, his cheeks hollowing as he sucked the head, pulling a heartfelt groan from him.

When Angelo eased Rick's length from his mouth, Rick whimpered in disappointment. Angelo grinned as he sucked on a couple of fingers until they were dripping, and then reached past Rick's balls to slide then through his crease. When Angelo took his shaft deep once more and pushed a slick finger into his arse, Rick cried out. Holding onto the headboard, he set up a rhythm as he pushed into Angelo's willing mouth and then pushed back, riding that finger, rocking between the two. When one finger became two, the sensations were suddenly more intense. Those black eyes were focused on him as Angelo slowly fucked him with his mouth and fingers. Rick synchronized his breathing to his thrusts, keeping it slow.

Angelo pulled free of Rick's body and sat up against the headboard, knees bent. Rick leaned back, Angelo's legs supporting him, and reached behind him to grasp the thick cock which rose up, rubbing insistently over his hole. Now it was Angelo's turn to moan softly. Rick became still, his gaze trained on Angelo's face. For a moment they regarded each other, their laboured breathing the only sound in the quiet room.

Without a word Rick leaned across to his bedside table, opened the top drawer and then took out a condom and his bottle of lube. Angelo watched him, lips parted, as Rick tore open the foil to remove the condom. He lifted himself up onto his knees and handed it to Angelo, who reached between Rick's spread thighs. He heard the snap of the latex as Angelo covered his cock and then took the lube from him. He listened to the sound of Angelo slicking himself up. Angelo laid a gentle hand on his hip and pulled him lower to where his cock waited. And then there was that glorious, heart-stopping moment when Angelo eased his dick into Rick's hole, slowly pushing up with his hips until Rick's arse met his thighs, cock snug inside him.

Rick shuddered out a breath as he rested there for several seconds, loving the wonderful feeling of having Angelo buried deep in his channel.

"Rick, look at me."

Rick's eyes met his, pupils blown, lips parted.

Angelo smiled. "That's it, look at me." He stared up at his lover as he tilted his hips and pushed up inside him, the motion fluid and exquisitely slow. Then Rick rolled his hips, taking Angelo deeper. Angelo groaned, the sound pulled from him as he kept the movement slow and sensual. He reached up to pull Rick down into a kiss, one hand cupping Rick's nape, the other languidly stroking the small of his back. Rick moaned into his mouth with each stroke of Angelo's cock inside him. Angelo ran his hand over the globe of Rick's arse, squeezing the firm flesh, before moving upward to rest on his shoulder, pressing Rick down onto him.

No words, only sounds, because no words were needed. They stared into each other's eyes, both focused intently on the other, the movement slow and sweet. Angelo didn't break eye contact, not once. The sensual rhythm, their synchronized breathing, the soft noises that spoke of building desire… it was hypnotic.

When Rick broke eye contact to roll back his head and utter a groan that reverberated through Angelo's body, Angelo knew it was time.

He pulled out and eased Rick onto his back, before grabbing a leg and hoisting it up over his shoulder. He pushed back inside and slid into the welcoming heat and softness that was Rick. And then he began to move.

Rick's breathing sped up. He stared down to where their bodies joined as Angelo thrust into him, building speed. Rick's eyes widened and Angelo knew he'd hit his mark.

"There," Rick demanded, voice quavering, and he grabbed onto Angelo's arse, pulling him deeper still. Angelo hooked his arms under both Rick's legs and fucked him faster, cock sliding into him as far as it could go. Rick reached down to tug at his dick, crying out each time Angelo's dick connected with his prostate. "Oh fuck, I'm so close."

With a roar Angelo thrust into him, hips snapping forward as he pushed them both toward orgasm. Rick was shaking, trembling uncontrollably. Angelo felt Rick's body tighten around him, gripping his cock in the molten heat of his channel. He pulled virtually all the way out and then fucked into him, grunting with the effort.

Rick came, hot seed pulsing out of his cock over their bodies, his mouth wide with a soundless cry. Angelo howled as Rick's tight arse milked him, pulling him into his own white-hot orgasm. He grabbed Rick's head and pulled him into a fierce kiss, both men gasping as Angelo shot his load deep inside Rick. Rick held onto him, their lips fused in a searing kiss as they were buffeted by wave upon wave of ecstasy.

Angelo collapsed onto Rick, skin damp with perspiration. He kissed his face and neck, moaning softly when Rick cupped his cheek and kissed him slowly and thoroughly. Angelo rocked him gently, his dick still inside Rick.

He didn't want it to end.

Chapter Fifteen

"What are you thinking?" Angelo asked him, as they lay cuddled up together on the couch. Sunday evening was ticking itself away, and Angelo desperately clung to the last remnants of a wonderful weekend.

Rick stretched like a cat, a contented sigh on his lips. "That being your lover isn't good for my health." He rolled onto his back and pulled Angelo on top of him, arms and legs coming up to wrap around him.

Angelo chuckled. "How do you work that out?" He wriggled delightedly at the feel of Rick's growing erection beneath him. He glanced at the clock. *Five minutes,* he thought with an inward grin. *Maybe less.*

Rick snickered. "Because we've existed all weekend on a diet of takeaway food, fast food, alcohol... need I go on?" He pushed up with his hips and Angelo let out a tiny moan of pleasure.

He dropped his head to speak softly into Rick's ear. "We've existed on a diet of something else, too." Rick shivered and Angelo kissed his ear, loving the way Rick squirmed under him, that cock growing harder by the second. He slid his lips over soft skin to Rick's neck, kissing the one little spot he'd found that made Rick lose it every time he went there.

Rick whimpered and his hips moved faster. Hands reached for Angelo's borrowed sweatpants and tugged them off impatiently. Angelo pulled off his T-shirt and pulled down Rick's shorts. No words, just breathless sounds. Angelo reached for one of the condoms on the coffee table and rolled it down over

Rick's rigid dick. After two days of nearly nonstop lovemaking, they'd learned their lesson well. There were condoms and lube in every room.

Without bothering to remove Rick's shorts, Angelo slicked up the hard dick that throbbed in his hand and then positioned himself, sinking down onto it with a groan as he welcomed Rick back into his body with ease. He glanced at the clock. Three minutes.

He grinned. *Damn, I'm good.*

Rick turned his face upward into the spray from the shower and closed his eyes, letting the warm water cascade down his body. He moaned quietly as two soapy hands reached around from behind him, moving over his chest. He let his head roll back to rest against Angelo's shoulder and sighed.

"*Now* I know why I asked you to stay last night. This is the perfect way to start a Monday morning— having my own personal slave wash me."

Angelo chuckled as he moved his hands lower to slide over Rick's cock which was already heavy and full. "Slaves have other uses, too," he whispered into Rick's ear.

Rick turned to face his lover, arms coming up to loop around Angelo's neck. He grinned. "Oh? Do tell."

Angelo kissed him, softly at first, but with growing passion, until Rick panted, hole clenching. He knew what was coming.

"Slaves are also required to service their masters, aren't they?" Angelo licked a line down Rick's throat, sucking and nipping here and there as he pressed Rick against the tiled wall.

Rick watched, licking his lips, as Angelo reached up to the glass shelf where he kept the shampoo, body wash and soap, and picked up a familiar foil-wrapped object. He laughed as Angelo ripped it open and hurriedly stretched the condom over his rock-hard cock. "Oh, you wicked man. You planned this."

Angelo grinned. "What—are you saying you're *objecting* to a good, hard, hot fuck in the shower before work?"

Anything Rick had been about to say was lost when Angelo bent his knees and picked Rick up, legs hooked over his arms, and then shoved him up against the wall. Rick gasped.

"Put it in you," Angelo ground out. Rick reached down and placed the head of Angelo's cock against his still-slick hole, easing it inside. He sighed as Angelo slowly pushed up into him until he was balls deep.

"Hold on tight, babe." Rick's eyes met his and Angelo grinned. "I did say a good, hard, hot fuck, remember?"

Rick grabbed onto his shoulders, and then cried out as Angelo fucked up into him with powerful thrusts, slamming into him, harsh grunts punctuating every thrust.

"Oh *fuck!*" Angelo was hammering his prostate. Every. Single. Fucking. Time.

"Come for me!" Angelo cried out, his abs rubbing against Rick's dick, creating a delicious friction between them.

And that was all it took to have Rick coming with a howl, balls high and tight, cock spurting come even as Angelo emptied his balls into the latex encasing him.

Rick was late to work.

Rick couldn't stop smiling.

Work was good. Actually, work was great, especially when he went into the kitchen to grab a coffee and discovered a plate of homemade chocolate chip cookies and a handwritten sign, *Help yourself - Lizzie.* Rick grinned. He *loved* days like these.

Especially when they begin with a hot man fucking me in the shower.

"Oh my God, Rick Wentworth, you are positively *glowing!*"

Rick faced Lizzie, mouth full of cookie. He swallowed and then smiled. "I might say the same thing about you." Lizzie looked radiant. "I take it things are going well with Dave?"

Lizzie beamed. "Things are going *very* well with Dave, thank you for asking." She walked over to where he stood by the coffee machine. "Just between us?" She sighed. "I think I'm in love."

Rick's heart melted. "Oh Lizzie, that's great." He leaned in close and whispered. "I know exactly how you feel."

Her eyes widened. "Angelo?" He nodded, unable to keep the gleeful smile from his face. Lizzie's smile broadened. "Oh, Rick, that's wonderful." She hugged him tight.

"Oh Gawd, jus' look at the pair o' you," Ed said with a groan. "Talk about loved up."

Lizzie extricated herself from Rick's embrace,

her cheeks flushing. "I'll talk to you later, okay, Rick?" She scooted out of the kitchen in a hurry, passing Blake as he entered.

Ed snorted. "So yer not denyin' it, then?"

"Denying what?" Blake asked as he helped himself to a coffee.

Ed pointed to Rick. "Rick 'ere is in love." He grinned mischievously. Blake's eyes widened.

Oh, fuck it. Rick couldn't hold it in any longer. "So what if I am?"

Ed's face unexpectedly broke into a rapturous smile. "'bout bleedin' time."

Rick cracked up laughing. He'd never been this happy in his life. He felt as if joy was bubbling up through him, about to burst out of him at any second.

If this is what it feels like to be in love? I'll take it.

He winked at Blake and then turned to Ed. "Now all we need to do now is find someone for you."

Ed barked out a laugh. "Yeah, an' good luck wi' that, mate. Me and the fairer sex don't tend to last too long these days."

Rick waggled his eyebrows. "Maybe you're working with the wrong plumbing, ever thought of that?" He smiled sweetly.

Blake snorted violently and Ed elbowed him in the stomach. "Quiet, you."

Rick gazed with interest at Ed's suddenly flushed cheeks. *Intriguing.* What made it even more intriguing was when Ed made his excuses and left in a hurry.

Blake bit back a smirk. He tapped his watch. "Back to work, you."

Rick chuckled to himself as he left the kitchen and went back to his office.

Yeah, he loved days like these.

Rick leaned back against his front door, his arms around Angelo and melted in his kiss. As they parted, he sighed.

"That was the perfect end to my day," he said, smiling. "Thank you." Angelo turning up at the office to take him to dinner had been a delightful surprise. They hadn't gone far, only a local pub which served a fantastic homemade steak and kidney pie, but it was exactly what Rick had needed.

"Oh, you're welcome," Angelo said. "But I meant what I said. I'm going to go back to my place tonight."

Rick pulled a face. "Aw, why?" He slid his arms down to grab Angelo's arse. "I could make it worth your while." He leered.

Angelo chortled. "Listen, you horny little beast, *you* may not be suffering any ill-effects from our weekend, but *I* certainly am." When Rick frowned, he leaned close to whisper in his ear. "I am absolutely *knackered*, babe. And *you* have to be feeling at least a *little* bit sore."

Rick was about to deny it, when Angelo reached down and rubbed a finger down the seam of his pants, pushing into his crease. Rick winced and Angelo smiled smugly.

Rick grumbled under his breath. "Okay, smug git." Angelo cackled. "Then you'd better go home and get some sleep, take some vitamins, whatever it takes. Because I am *not* going to wait until the weekend before you and I get down 'n' dirty again. Do you hear me?" He grinned.

Angelo took him in his arms and kissed him tenderly. When they broke apart, he gave Rick a sweet little kiss on the tip of his nose. "Sleep well, babe. I'll talk to you soon." He gave him one of those smiles that always made Rick warm inside, and then walked toward the elevator. As the doors slid open he gave Rick one last wave before he disappeared from view.

Rick let himself into the flat and glanced around, recalling some of the things they'd gotten up to that weekend. *That* brought a smile to his face. Then he sighed as a line from an old song came to mind.

Ricky's in love.

Nope. Not denying it. At. All.

Something buzzed. Bloody insistently. And it was pissing Rick off.

He opened his eyes and gazed blearily at the LED clock by his bed. It was eleven o'clock.

I've only been in bed for an hour. He'd decided to follow Angelo's example and get an early night. He'd wanted to say goodnight to his boyfriend but Angelo wasn't answering his phone. *He's probably fallen asleep on the couch, worn out.* In spite of his fatigue, Rick smiled to himself at the thought of Angelo, exhausted from too much sex.

And something was still buzzing. It was his phone.

Rick was now wide awake. He grabbed the phone and lay back against his pillows. He grinned when he saw Angelo's number. *Ah, he's woken up.* He connected the call and started speaking. "Don't tell me—you fell asleep in front of the TV, yeah?"

"Is that Rick?" It was a female voice.

Rick sat bolt upright in bed. "Who is this?"

"If you're Rick, then you need to listen," she said urgently. "My name is Maria Tarallo. I'm Angelo's sister."

Cold fingers wrapped around his heart and squeezed. "What's happened?"

"I'm at St. Thomas's hospital. Angelo has been beaten up."

The world suddenly came to a dizzying stop. "Oh my God. How bad is it?" He leaped out of bed and then reached for his clothes, phone pressed against his ear. "Never mind, I'm on my way." He disconnected the call and then scrambled into his jeans and sweater as fast as he could. *What the hell happened?*

He was out of the apartment block and into a passing taxi within ten minutes. Rick's stomach rolled as he called his mother. He knew there was little chance of his parents being asleep. When she answered, he told her the little he knew, and promised to call when he had more information.

"We won't be able to sleep until we hear from you, you know that." He could hear her concern. He assured her he'd call. Then he tried to call Blake, but there was no answer, and the same result for Will. Rick left messages and then switched off his phone as the hospital came into view. He threw some money at the driver and then dashed into Reception.

When he was informed Angelo was in ICU, a wave of dizziness and nausea rolled over him. All the way up in the elevator, he kept telling himself that it was going to be fine, repeating it over and over again, talking it into existence. When he caught sight of the young woman by the desk in the Intensive Care Unit, he knew she had to be Maria. Her resemblance to Angelo was obvious.

Maria attempted a relieved smile when he approached her. "I'd know you anywhere."

The remark puzzled him but there was a far more pressing matter to deal with. "Where is he? And what's wrong with him?"

She beckoned him to follow. "He's along here. The hospital called me on his phone. They said he was found not far from his studio, unconscious. He's got injuries to his head and a broken leg, a compound fracture, I think. But the most serious thing is that he's unconscious."

Rick froze and came to a dead stop in the middle of the hallway. "How long has he been like this?" A huge rock sat on his chest, making it difficult to breathe.

Maria took his hand. "They think it's something to do with his head injuries," she said and then swallowed. Now that he looked closely, he could see the fear in her eyes. "The doctors have told me he's breathing by himself, he just can't wake up. They're observing him constantly." She knocked on the glass door and a nurse punched into a keypad to let them enter.

"This is Rick, Angelo's partner," she explained to the nurse.

Rick gave her a grateful look. She squeezed his hand and led him to the bed in the corner of the wide unit. There were several beds, but only two were occupied. Rick let out a low gasp as he caught sight of Angelo, his leg already in plaster and suspended from a frame. Next to his bed, the quiet beep of the heart monitor was a reassuring sound. An intravenous drip was in place.

Angelo looked for all the world as if he were sleeping. Rick approached the bed and leaning over, he kissed him gently on the forehead. "Hi there, babe." The sight of Angelo's face, bruised and battered, brought tears to his eyes. He took Angelo's hand in his. The skin was cool to the touch. He bent low and kissed Angelo's fingers. When he straightened, he found Maria standing at the foot of the bed, staring at them. Her dark eyes, so reminiscent of Angelo's, were large and round.

"You love my brother."

Rick smiled. It got easier each time he said it. "Yeah, I love him." He glanced around. "Is anyone else coming from your family?"

She nodded. "I rang my brothers and my parents. They're on their way."

A tapping on the glass had them both turning toward the door. Maria exhaled. "That's Luca."

The nurse let him in and Luca rushed across to the bed, his face paling as he saw Angelo.

"I got here as fast as I could," he explained. "What happened to him?" He caught sight of Rick and stiffened. "I know who you are," he said with a sneer.

Maria hit him across the arm, hard. "You have more important things to concern you right now. Forget your own ignorant prejudices for a moment and concentrate on our brother."

His face fell. "What happened to him?" he repeated softly.

"The ambulance crew who treated him spoke with witnesses. They said he was beaten up by a gang of four or five men," she said, pain etched across her face. When she told Luca about the head injuries and the resulting, almost comatose, state, Luca's eyes widened.

He stared at Angelo, aghast. "Will he wake up?" he asked quietly.

The nurse walked up to do Angelo's observations. "All the signs are that he'll come round," she told Luca. "The only thing we cannot predict with any degree of accuracy is when."

Luca nodded, his gaze fixed on Angelo.

Rick's throat was suddenly dry. "Is there anywhere around here where I can get something to drink?"

Maria smiled. "There's a drinks machine around the corner. I was about to get one myself, so I'll come with you." She turned to her brother. "Do you want something, Luca?"

Luca frowned. "What? Oh. No, I'm fine." He appeared extremely distracted. In spite of his anger at how Luca had treated Angelo, Rick felt himself softening toward the older man. *He must care for his brother, even if he* is *an idiot*, he thought.

"Come on." Maria tugged at his arm. "Let's go find you a hot drink." She glanced at her brother. "I'm sure Angelo will be okay for a moment."

Nodding, he followed her from the ICU. Sure enough, there was the drinks machine. He fumbled through his pocket for loose change and bought two hot chocolates. Maria thanked him as he handed one to her.

They walked slowly back along the corridor in silence. The hospital was quiet. Rick looked at his watch and stared. It was nearly midnight. He'd lost all track of time.

As they neared the corridor which led to ICU, he heard a raised voice. It was Luca.

Oh my God, something's happened to Angelo. He was about to break into a run when Maria caught hold of his arm, stopping him. He opened his mouth to speak but she held up a finger to her lips. Her face was white.

"What the fuck did you think you were playing at?" Luca said in a low voice. Silence. "Well, he's still fucking unconscious, that's how bad it is." More silence. "I didn't ask you to do a fucking thing!"

Rick felt sick. *What the hell?*

"I don't care if you thought you were doing me a favour. I should never have told you about Angelo in the first place." Silence. Luca let out a low growl. "Okay, so he may be a fag, but he's still my brother, you moron. And if he wakes up and identifies you and the old Bill come calling round, they're gonna think I had something to do with this."

A wave of dizziness swept over Rick and he lurched into a nearby trolley, sending it crashing into the wall and spilling his hot drink, nearly scalding himself in the process. Maria caught hold of him.

"Look, I gotta go. But this is not over."

Rick heard the chiming of the keypad to ICU, and then silence. He waited until he was sure Luca had entered the unit, and then turned to Maria. "What the fuck was that all about?"

Maria's nostrils flared. "Let's go find out, shall we?" Her expression was unreadable as they walked around the corner and up to the door of ICU. The nurse let them in.

Rick walked over to where Luca stood beside the bed, gazing down at his brother, an anguished expression on his face. Rick was about to confront him but Maria stopped him.

"This one is mine," she said grimly.

And then she walked up to Luca and drove her fist into his solar plexus.

Luca dropped like a stone.

Chapter Sixteen

"You bastard!" Maria said in a low voice as Luca lay doubled up on the floor, groaning in pain. "This is all your fault! And don't try to deny it, because we heard you."

"Is there something wrong?"

Rick looked around quickly to see the nurse approaching, her expression alarmed when she caught sight of Luca. "Are you all right?" she asked.

Luca got up off the floor, white as a sheet, arms wrapped around his middle. "I'm fine," he said, a little breathless. "I tripped up. I'll be okay in a minute."

The nurse looked doubtful, but Luca managed to paste on a reassuring smile. She gave him one last look and then went back to her other patient.

Luca glared at his sister, arms still crossed. "I don't know what you're talking about," he said in a low voice.

"Don't lie to me!" Maria advanced on him, fist clenched. Rick was impressed. Angelo's little sister was a spitfire when roused.

Luca held up his hands. "Okay, okay. But it was nothing to do with me, honest. I had no idea."

Maria took a step closer. "Keep talking."

Luca took a deep breath. "Look, I mouthed off to some of my mates about Angelo a few weeks ago. They were sympathizing with me, about having a fa—" He broke off, eyes meeting Rick's for the first time. Rick met his gaze with a cool stare. Luca's cheeks were suddenly bright red and he looked away. "Anyway, it seems they thought they'd do me a favour by teaching my brother a lesson. They jumped him on his way into his studio and beat the shit out of him." His troubled gaze alighted on Angelo. "Only they went too far."

"Too far?" Maria mimicked. "Luca, they put him in a coma!" Her mouth tightened. "You're going to call the police and tell them everything."

Luca's eyes widened. "I can't. These are my mates."

Maria growled. "And this is your brother. Put it this way. If you don't call them, *I* will—and I will name you as an accessory."

It was evident from Luca's face that he believed her. Hell, *Rick* believed her in that moment. Luca nodded reluctantly and Maria let out her breath. Her fist unclenched.

The nurse came over. "Your parents are here," she said quietly. "We don't have the normal visiting rules in here about the number of visitors, but I must ask that you all keep the noise level to a minimum, all right?"

They nodded. Rick looked toward the glass door. Angelo's mother had obviously been crying. Her face was puffy and blotchy. His father looked white-faced with shock. The nurse brought them over to the bed where they stared at their son, aghast, as she filled them in on Angelo's condition. Angelo's mother started crying, but his father said nothing. He didn't acknowledge Rick's presence.

Maria regarded her father steadily. "You nearly lost your son tonight."

Her father jerked his head up and stared at her, clearly startled. Rick saw pain in his eyes.

Maria's face was sad. "But you've lost him

anyway, because he's chosen Rick, Dad. The man he loves." His face tightened. "Is this what you want, Dad? Look at him. If you force him to marry a girl, you're condemning him and whoever he marries—and any kids—to a life of unhappiness." She glanced at Angelo, her chin trembling. "And Angelo's injuries are all due to the actions of people who think just... like... you." Maria glared at her brother. "Aren't they, Luca?"

Luca froze. His father observed him closely. "What do you know about this?"

Luca looked from his father to his brother, lying there so still, oblivious to the drama taking place around him. Rick stood by the side of the bed and watched the play of emotions on Luca's expression. Luca's face crumpled and he broke. Stammering, tears trickling down his cheeks, Luca told his father everything. Although there wasn't a mean bone in his body, Rick found it difficult to feel sympathy for him. Luca's tears worsened when a look of horror etched itself on his father's face.

Luca raised wet eyes full of misery and gazed at his sister. "You're right, he's still my brother." He glanced across at Rick. "I'm sorry for how I spoke to you earlier. You didn't deserve that." He gulped. "After all, you're here because you care about him too."

Rick was stunned. Maria walked over to Rick and put her arms around him. "My brother is lucky to have you." She hugged him tightly. Rick closed his eyes, grateful for the contact.

Angelo's mother came over to the opposite side of the bed and stroked Angelo's forehead and then down his arm which lay on top of the sheet.

His father stood at the foot of the bed, silent, his gaze fixed on his immobile son. Then he glanced at Rick and gave him a brief, tight nod. Rick stared back for a moment, too dazed to react. He flashed Angelo's father a quick smile.

"Dad, why don't you and Luca go and get some coffee for everyone?" Maria suggested. "We might be here for a while, and I for one could use some caffeine right now."

Her father regarded her steadily and then beckoned Luca with a flick of his head. "Come on, let's go find some coffee, son." The two men walked out of ICU.

Angelo's mother sat in a chair on one side of the bed, Rick and Maria on the other, Maria's arm draped around Rick's shoulders.

Rick stared at his lover, willing him silently to wake up.

You have a great sister, babe. Wait till you hear how she spoke to your father. You'd be so proud of her.

Then something occurred to him. Didn't they say people in comas were aware of what was going on around them? It was worth a try.

He leaned in close and spoke quietly to his lover. "Find your way back to me, baby. I need you."

He prayed Angelo heard him.

⚜

Angelo slowly opened his eyes, and then regretted it. His head ached like a bastard. He winced at the light which shone down on him from above his bed.

Wait a minute—I don't have a light above my bed.

Where in the hell am I? And come to think of it, I ache all over.

He peered around him, moving his head carefully. The first thing he saw was his parents, dozing in two chairs across from his bed. He frowned. *I get it—I'm dreaming. This is some surreal dream.* Then he became aware of a hand clutching his. He glanced down to find Rick asleep, his head on the bed, their hands intertwined. Angelo stared at Rick for a moment or two, gazing at the ruffled brown hair, the shadow of stubble on his cheeks, the regular sound of his breathing. He squeezed Rick's hand gently.

Rick slowly opened his eyes and blinked. Then he jerked his head off the bed and stared at Angelo, his face breaking into a beautiful smile. "Oh my God. You're awake."

Angelo let out a bemused chuckle. "Sure I'm awake. It's bloody difficult to sleep with that light on." Rick moved up the bed to kiss him softly on the lips, hand cupping his cheek tenderly. Angelo sighed, melting into the sweet embrace. When they parted, he gazed into Rick's eyes. "I'm glad you're here. Except…where is here? What happened? Last thing I remember was someone hitting me in the back of the head. And what time is it?"

Rick became still. "You were assaulted last night, by four or five men. And it's nearly dawn. You've been unconscious ever since."

Angelo could only stare at him, unable to take it in. Then he caught sight of his leg, set in a plaster cast. *Oh, bloody hell.*

Rick rang the bell above Angelo's bed. Within the space of a minute a nurse appeared by the bed, beaming when she saw Angelo. Rick released his hand to stand back while the nurse checked him out, making notes on his chart.

"Glad to have you back with us, Angelo," she said quietly. "Now get some rest, please." She levelled a firm stare in Rick's direction. "He needs to sleep."

Rick nodded. "Message received and understood."

She gave him an approving nod and walked off.

"Angelo?" His mother was awake. He watched her shake his father. Angelo stiffened. Dad was the last person he wanted to speak with.

His parents got up out of their chairs and came across to him. Mum kissed him on the cheek. "Oh, thank God." She ran her fingers through his hair, her hand trembling. She smiled at him, eyes shining. "Hi there. You had us all so worried."

Angelo touched her face gently. "Hi, Mum." He looked to where his father stood beside his mother. "Dad." He acknowledged his presence, but that was as far as he was willing to go.

"Son, do you know what happened to you?"

Angelo frowned. "Apparently I was beaten up but I have no recollection of it, beyond receiving a blow to the back of my head."

His father sighed. "Then you need to know something." As he told Angelo what had happened, Angelo went cold, especially when he heard that it had been Luca's friends. His brother was nowhere to be seen.

"Where is Luca?" he gritted out. "Too ashamed to face me? How the hell could he be involved in something like this?" He couldn't get his head round it. His own fucking brother. Angelo's head throbbed.

"Hey, wait a minute there." Rick was back by his

side in an instant. He grasped Angelo's hand in his. He gazed at Angelo, his brow furrowed. "Luca didn't know. He really wasn't part of it." Rick spoke earnestly. "Your parents sent him and Maria home to get some sleep. He's very upset." He squeezed Angelo's hand. "Besides, you can't blame him for having dickheads for friends."

Angelo caught the look of surprise on his father's face.

The nurse appeared by the bed. "Two gentlemen have arrived, asking to see Angelo and Rick." She frowned. "I really shouldn't let them in at this hour but they're being very insistent."

Angelo wondered who they could be. "Please let them come in. I promise we'll keep it quiet." He gazed at her appealingly. She sighed and finally nodded before going to admit his mystery guests.

Rick shook his head, clearly trying not to laugh. "Angelo Tarallo, did you just flash puppy dog eyes at that nurse?"

Angelo's cheeks heated up. Then he stared in surprise at the sight of Rick's boss, Blake Davis, and another guy, both in tuxedos. They walked straight up to Rick and hugged him before turning to speak to everyone else.

"Sorry for coming here at this hour," Blake apologized to them, "but we were attending a party for the release of Michael Davenport's latest book, and I only switched my phone on about thirty minutes ago and saw Rick's message. We got here as fast as we could." He beamed when he saw Angelo. "Oh thank God, you're awake." He came up to the bed and squeezed Angelo's hand. "It's good to see you again." His companion joined him. "This is my fiancé, Will."

Angelo greeted Will with a brief nod. Then he tilted his head. "Michael Davenport?"

Blake nodded. "He's one of our most prolific authors and the party just kept on going."

Blake went over to his parents and extended his hand, introducing himself and Will. Angelo couldn't help but notice that his father seemed impressed, and more than a little surprised. Blake and Will came across as two very confident men who were clearly not in the least bit embarrassed about their sexuality. Angelo had to wonder if his father even knew any gay men. He doubted it.

A wave of fatigue washed over him, and he yawned, suddenly aware of his aching body.

"You need to sleep, babe." Rick's reaction was instantaneous. Angelo gave him a grateful smile. Rick turned to their visitors. "Thanks, everyone, for being here, but Angelo needs to rest now.

Will smiled. "I think that's our cue to leave, isn't it?" He addressed Rick. "We'll drop you off at home."

Rick shook his head. "I'm not going anywhere." Angelo reached for Rick's hand and squeezed it gently.

"I don't want to see you at the office, okay? At least for a few days," Blake told Rick, a mock stern look on his face. Rick grinned and nodded. Will and Blake shook hands with his parents, before hugging Rick and saying goodbye to him. They left the unit.

"We'll say goodnight, then. Or good morning, rather." His father stood at the foot of the bed, hands gripping the bed rail. Angelo regarded him for a moment and then nodded. His mother came up to him, fussing, but Dad took hold of her arm and steered her toward the door. Angelo waved her goodbye.

Rick sat down on the edge of his bed, chuckling. "Your father had to practically push your mother out of the door."

Angelo stretched out a hand to him, and Rick edged closer, bending down to kiss him softly on the lips. Angelo sighed into the kiss. "I'm so glad you're here."

Rick smiled. "Like I said. I'm not going anywhere."

Thank God for that.

Rick locked eyes with him. "Love you."

Angelo's heart skipped a beat at hearing those words for the first time from Rick's lips. Carefully, he pulled Rick toward and kissed him, nice and slow, before bringing their foreheads together. Angelo drank in Rick's warm, comforting scent.

"I love you, too."

Two months later

Rick caught the animated chatter from the lounge and grinned. The football match on TV seemed to be going well, going by the loud comments and shouts of Angelo, his brothers and his father. He added seasoning and then stirred the sauce before trying it. *Perfect.*

"Is it ready?" Angelo's mother Elena asked as she came to stand beside him at the stove.

Rick dipped the spoon into the sauce and held it out to her. "Have a taste."

She blew on the hot liquid and then tasted it. "Oh, now that is *good*, Rick. And those meatballs you brought with you smell wonderful. What's in them?"

He winked. "My secret ingredient."

Elena put her hand to her chest, a look of mock hurt on her face. "And you're not going to share it with *me*?"

Rick chuckled and whispered in her ear. "Caraway seeds." She smiled.

A cheer rose in the lounge and Rick grinned. "Chelsea have scored, I see." He turned off the heat and put a lid on the saucepan.

"The table's set." Paolo's wife Tina appeared in the kitchen doorway.

"Where's Elsa?" Elena asked her.

"She's in the garden with all the kids. Oh, and she's volunteered to sit in the kitchen with the kids for lunch."

Rick laughed at that. "Well, three of them are hers."

Elena snickered. "Go get everyone to the table, please, Tina." Her daughter-in-law nodded and disappeared. Between the two of them, they put all the food into serving dishes and carried them through into the Tarallos' dining room. Then he and Elena set out the children's lunches. Rick laughed at the sight of four little boys and two girls, all of differing ages and sizes, clamouring to sit around Elena's round kitchen table. He grinned at Elsa, who had apparently drawn the short straw, before following Elena into the dining room.

Angelo's father Vittorio came into the room with three bottles of red wine which he'd already opened. The rest of the family, ten people in all, came to sit around the large oak table, Angelo at the end so he had room for his leg in its cast. Rick sat down next to him.

"When's the cast coming off, Angelo?"

Angelo groaned. "The first one was on for six weeks, but the doc says maybe this one won't be as long. I can't wait, 'cause it itches like bloody hell." Elena gave him a look and he squirmed. "Sorry, Mum." She totally spoiled the effect by grinning at him. There was a buzz of chatter as the family began helping themselves to pasta, meatballs, sauce, salad and fresh bread. Vittorio went around the table, pouring out the wine.

Angelo leaned close to Rick and spoke quietly into his ear. "I can't wait 'til it comes off and I can move back to my own house."

Rick smiled. "Well, I did offer to have you stay with me, but your mother didn't want you on your own while I was at work." He stroked Angelo's jean-encased thigh. "Poor baby."

"I can't even find enough privacy around here for a wank," Angelo grumbled.

Rick chuckled. "Do you need some help with that later?"

Angelo's eyes were hot. "Always. And that's another thing—God, I miss you."

Rick squeezed his thigh gently. "Not long now, baby. And then we'll have all the time we want to be together." Angelo's eyes locked on his, and Rick felt a shiver run through him.

"I'd like to propose a toast." Vittorio stood at the end of the table, glass in hand. "Here's to having all of my family around me, all together under one roof. And for this wonderful meal, my thanks to the cooks, Mama and Rick."

Elena and Rick reached across the table and high-fived. Everyone burst out laughing except Maria who huffed. "What am I, chopped liver?"

Elena smiled sweetly at her daughter. "Oh darling, the salad is nice and you sliced up the bread beautifully." Another burst of laughter echoed around the room, and Maria joined in this time.

Vittorio regarded the people assembled around his table. "It's good to have *all* my family here." Rick saw a look pass between Vittorio and Elena before Vittorio caught Angelo's eye. Angelo gave his father a brief nod.

Luca smiled. "Here, here."

Rick reached for Angelo's hand and held it tightly. *Love you,* he mouthed.

Angelo's eyes shone. *Love you too.*

The End

About the author

K.C. Wells lives on an island off the south coast of the UK, surrounded by natural beauty. She writes about men who love men, and can't even contemplate a life that doesn't include writing.

The rainbow rose tattoo on her back with the words 'Love is Love' and 'Love Wins' is her way of hoisting a flag. She plans to be writing about men in love - be it sweet and slow, hot or kinky - for a long while to come.

Available titles

Learning to Love
Michael & Sean
Evan & Daniel
Josh & Chris
Final Exam

Sensual Bonds
A Bond of Three
A Bond of Truth

Merrychurch Mysteries
Truth Will Out
Roots of Evil
A Novel Murder

Love, Unexpected
Debt
Burden

Dreamspun Desires
The Senator's Secret
Out of the Shadows
My Fair Brady
Under The Covers

Lions & Tigers & Bears
A Growl, a Roar, and a Purr

Love Lessons Learned
First
Waiting for You
Step by Step
Bromantically Yours

BFF

Collars & Cuffs
An Unlocked Heart
Trusting Thomas
Someone to Keep Me (K.C. Wells & Parker Williams)
A Dance with Domination
Damian's Discipline (K.C. Wells & Parker Williams)
Make Me Soar
Dom of Ages (K.C. Wells & Parker Williams)
Endings and Beginnings (K.C. Wells & Parker Williams)

Secrets – with Parker Williams
Before You Break
An Unlocked Mind
Threepeat
On the Same Page

Personal
Making it Personal
Personal Changes
More than Personal
Personal Secrets
Strictly Personal
Personal Challenges

Personal – The Complete Series

Confetti, Cake & Confessions

Connections

Saving Jason
A Christmas Promise
The Law of Miracles
My Christmas Spirit
A Guy for Christmas

Island Tales
Waiting for a Prince
September's Tide
Submitting to the Darkness

Lightning Tales
Teach Me
Trust Me
See Me
Love Me

A Material World
Lace
Satin
Silk
Denim

Southern Boys
Truth & Betrayal
Pride & Protection
Desire & Denial

Kel's Keeper
Here For You
Sexting The Boss
Gay on a Train
Sunshine & Shadows
Watch and Learn
Double or Nothing

Back from the Edge
Lose to Win
Teasing Tim
Switching it up
Out for You
State of Mind
My Best Friend's Brother
Bears in the Woods

Anthologies

Fifty Gays of Shade
Winning Will's Heart

Come, Play
Watch and Learn

Writing as Tantalus
Damon & Pete: Playing with Fire

Made in the USA
Monee, IL
21 March 2022

93266509R10125